THE WEST OF
ERNEST HAYCOX

A killer fought his worst enemy—fear . . .
One man faced the hate of a whole town . . .
A youth learned the bitter taste of Indian
vengeance . . .

Eleven magnificent episodes of the West, by
one of the great novelists of the West. "Few
men have known the West and its history as
well as Ernest Haycox." —THE NEW YORK TIMES

BY ERNEST HAYCOX

THE MAN FROM MONTANA

A DELL BOOK   An original Western

Published by DELL PUBLISHING CO., INC.
750 Third Avenue
New York 17, New York

Copyright © 1964, by Jill Marie Haycox

Dell ® TM 681510, Dell Publishing Co., Inc.

First printing—February, 1964

Printed in U.S.A.

ACKNOWLEDGMENTS: The following stories are published by permission
of Jill Marie Haycox and her agents, Scott Meredith Literary Agency,
Inc.:

THE MAN FROM MONTANA—Copyright 1927 by Doubleday, Page &
Company; Copyright renewed 1955 by Jill Marie Haycox.

GRASSHOPPER DANCE—Copyright 1938 by Jill Marie Haycox.

RODEO—Copyright 1932 by Benevolent & Protective Order of Elks of
the United States of America; Copyright renewed 1959 by Jill Marie
Haycox.

IMPORTANT QUESTION—Copyright 1938 by Jill Marie Haycox.

HANG UP MY GUN—Copyright 1932 by Street & Smith Corp.; Copyright
renewed 1959 by Jill Marie Haycox.

THE MISFIT—Copyright 1949 by Jill Marie Haycox.

DEEP WINTER—Copyright 1942 by Jill Marie Haycox.

PRIDE—Copyright 1934 by Doubleday Doran & Company, Inc.; Copyright renewed 1961 by Jill Marie Haycox.

GENTLEMEN STAND TOGETHER—Copyright 1936 by Jill Marie Haycox;
Copyright renewed 1964 by Jill Marie Haycox.

SECOND-MONEY MAN—Copyright 1933 by P. F. Collier & Son Company;
Copyright renewed 1960 by Jill Marie Haycox.

THE OUTCAST—Copyright 1958 by Jill Marie Haycox.

CONTENTS

THE MAN FROM
MONTANA

THE MAN FROM MONTANA

He was long of arm, slender of hip and his coat hung loosely across a pair of extraordinarily wide shoulders. In cattle land, economy of flesh is the invariable rule and this man was no exception; but even when he came riding into Bad News, dusty and weary and slouching forward in his saddle, he somehow gave the impression of a quick, slashing strength. He had a face boldly hewn, with the high-bridged nose terminating in a mouth habitually compressed. Blue eyes, sometimes sharp and aggressive, sometimes sad, looked straightforwardly upon the hot and shimmering horizon. But the most singular feature of the man was his hair, which was almost white; one might have called him old, and considering the span of active life among the roping and riding fraternity he was old. But there were men in Bad News who saw him come and watched him from between narrowed eyes as he strolled toward Dixon's House. And they were right when they said he was not far from thirty. As for his name, no one knew it; but he had not been in the cow town more than six hours before they were referring to him as Silver Top. And that name was the only one he answered to until the memorable night in Dixon's when he stood in the center of the dimly lit hall with gunsmoke trailing around him and the flash of fire in his eyes. Then, in a drawling, husky voice he introduced himself. "I'm Joe Lane, from Montana. I reckon you've been itchin' to know it. Now, damn you, turn over and die!"

But in the beginning no one knew where he came from, though many men for many different reasons were anxious to know and of these one particular man, Ab Deering, went to some pains to find out. It was Ab who sat on the porch of his Halfway Resort when the newcomer, coated with alkali dust, rode down the single dreary street with its battered, battlemented wooden shacks, and it was Ab who first paid attention to the man's long and slender fingers. They were the finely kept digits of an artist, and Ab's gaze dropped toward the newcomer's gunbelt—to discover that though there was a gunbelt, no holster and revolver swung from it. Ab's lids dropped, curtaining the harsh, slate-gray eyes; and through the narrow slit of vision he studied this traveler with redoubled interest, seeking among other things the tell-tale bulge under the armpit. But there was none and Ab pulled on his unlit cigar, wondering.

No stranger entering Bad News passed down that rutty street unobserved; for though the town seemed utterly dead, on the point of crumbling to fragments and blowing away, there were figures posted here and there—in the saloons, on the hotel porch, in obscure alleyways—who watched with a wariness of gaze that gave the direct lie to their studied indolence. Bad News slumbered under the sun and woke to hectic, brawling activity only after dark.

The newcomer rode on, looking directly ahead, aware of the inspection he was passing through; and without turning his head he saw Ab Deering and made note of Ab Deering's ape-like bulk. Made note, too, of the intent, predatory glance which the man fastened upon him. He filed it in his memory, lips compressing tighter. When he came to the livery stable he turned in, dismounted and removed his gear. Out of the half-shadows of the place came a man who walked grotesquely, bobbing up and down on a misshapen leg that bent with the pressure put on it. He was a thin, undernourished creature who looked upon the world with a morose, half defiant scowl and when he spoke it seemed as if he expected this traveler to treat him with the same veiled contempt that others had bestowed upon him. This was cattle land, the wildest, most free, most democratic land in the world, yet even here there was an aristocracy—that of a sound, active body. The traveler was of that aristocracy. A glance proved it and the stable roustabout's surliness grew more profound.

"Whadja want?"

The traveler's blue eyes went squarely to the other's face, with never a side glance at the roustabout's obvious infirmity. He was very grave and studiously polite. "I'd admire to have you put this animal in front of some hay, friend. I'm stayin' awhile."

"Oh," said the roustabout, unfriendliness melting.

"I reckon," drawled the newcomer, "the place across the street is where I want to bunk and eat, ain't it?"

"Dixon's House," affirmed the roustabout. "The grub is good and the beds is clean." He stood in his tracks, looking upward at the newcomer. Presently, some long suppressed need of sympathy rose to the surface. "Gawd, but I got a toothache!"

"Sho!" murmured the newcomer. "They're tough. Is it a good tooth?"

"Aw, hell no! It's been a killin' me five-six months. If they was a tooth yanker anywheres—"

The traveler nodded his head. "Don't pay to stand unnecessary misery. You got a pair of pliers around?"

The roustabout was on the point of refusing the service. But the straight blue eyes were weighing him and he ended by shuffling into a stall and finding something that resembled wire cutters. The two of them moved toward the light and the roustabout opened and closed his mouth uneasily. "It don't allus give me trouble," he explained.

The newcomer grinned and somehow its effect was to make the roustabout square his shoulders and say, "Aw, take the cussed thing out. I been bothered a-plenty."

"That's the spirit," observed the newcomer. The pliers explored around the roustabout's mouth, touching here and there. "Once," said the newcomer, "I knew a man in Billings who was about your build and was the dead image—that's the grinder, ain't it? Well, I'll just take an easy hold first to see if these things grip—Like I said, he was the dead image

11

of you. Got any brothers in Billings? Hang steady, friend. There she stands."

It was done. The roustabout fell back. "You ain't did it already? Well, I'll be singed! Say, you know how!"

"You said the hotel fellow's name was Dixon, didn't you?" queried the newcomer, drifting out. The roustabout rubbed his jaw and watched the man cross the street. He took a chew of tobacco and filled his chest. "You tell Dixon it's my treat, Silver Top!"

The newcomer's smile came back to him. "That's a good moniker. Thanks."

"He's an all right guy," muttered the roustabout to himself. "But if he's a-goin' to roost in these quarters he oughta be totin' a wee-pon. He shore oughta." Of a sudden, fine lines of worry formed around his mouth.

The sun dipped beyond the distant range and instantly it was twilight in the town. A small breeze scoured down the dusty street, bringing with it the pungent scent of sage. Back of the hotel somebody began to bang the kitchen triangle and men moved leisurely toward Dixon's. Silver Top walked across the porch into the place, feeling eyes upon him. At the counter there was an old man with a yellow beard and resolute shoulders.

"Welcome to Bad News," said he, inclining his head. "The room will be four bits and each meal likewise. I'm Theed Dixon and if you got any val'ables I'll lock 'em in my safe." The hotel man's hand swept proudly toward the safe against the wall, and Silver Top spent a long, curious glance upon it. "It's held a lot o' money and it ain't been cracked yet," reassured Dixon, noting the glance.

"Thanks," said Silver Top, smiling. "What ever made you think I carried anything worth puttin' in a safe? But I'm obliged for the compliment." He accepted the outstretched pen and bent over the hotel register, seeming to hestitate. In the end he wrote "Silver Top" and drawled, "That'll be ample, I reckon."

Dixon nodded and was about to speak when men began filing through into the dining room. Silver Top, half turned,

12

saw Ab Deering roll by, his squat, ugly body seeming to expand at each step. The man was built like a barrel and his skin was the color of burnt shoe-leather. A cowlick of greasy hair extended below his hat band and a celluloid toothpick protruded from a corner of his mouth. It seemed for an instant that he recognized the newcomer and that he was about to speak. Instead, he dropped his head and went on. Dixon looked quickly from one to the other and spoke, almost irritably. "You come on and I'll show you yore room."

The two walked up the stairs and down a dark corridor, stopping at a door. Dixon threw it open and tarried an instant. "It's a nice little town," said he.

Silver Top put a fraternal hand on Dixon's shoulder. "Spit it out, dad."

"Then," went on Dixon, dropping his voice, "you better put on yore gun. A man's bare naked 'thout one in these parts."

"What makes you think I need one?"

Dixon peered at the other's face. "I know a man when I see him."

Silver Top dropped his arm. There was a brittle quality in his voice. "I've quit wearin' hardware, dad. It's the devil's own device."

Dixon's mouth shut like a vise and he moved away. "Jus' so—jus' so. Nev'less, you'll have to choose."

"Choose what, dad?"

The hotel keeper shook his head and descended the stairs. Silver Top went into his room, closed the door softly and sat on the edge of his bed. For half an hour he rested, scarcely moving a muscle. But the lines of his face settled perceptibly and the light of his eyes grew greyer, blacker. "Have I got to fight that all over again?" he muttered. "Ain't a man got a right to any peace of mind in this world?" He began locking his fingers together and rubbing them gently, pressing them backward and forward in a kind of exercise. It was an involuntary gesture and presently he caught himself and looked upon the long and slender implements with grim

13

disfavor. "It's shore hard to get away from the old tricks."

The clatter from the dining room waxed and waned. The men of Bad News were quick feeders, and in a little while Silver Top heard them clumping out and into the street. The town began to revive as the night fell. For a space the newcomer debated getting his horse and riding away—as quietly as he came, seeking some remote place where he would be at peace with himself. The idea passed and in the end he rose and started down the stairs to eat. "A man can't be runnin' forever," he reflected. "I got to fight it out. By the Lord Harry, I got to! And it'll be right off the bat, too. For if there ain't a fine dish of trouble in this sink of depravity, all signs read wrong."

The dining room was deserted and he sat alone until a woman came from the kitchen and silently put a bowl of soup before him. It was quite dark in the room, but when he looked up at her, he saw the full-breasted, arrow-straight body tarrying beside his chair. In the shadows her face was blurred; a wide forehead glowed slightly beneath a heavy mass of hair and there was an ivory gleam at her throat. When she spoke it was in a soft, slurring accent. "Beef or spareribs, mister."

"I'll stick to cow," said he, matching her lazy drawl.

She moved away and it seemed to the newcomer there was a particular rhythm in the way she walked. A kerosene lamp flared under her hand and she brought it over and set it on the table. Of a sudden he found himself held by clear, gray eyes. There was a point of light flickering in them; otherwise she appeared to be holding herself away from the world, as if she were afraid to release the forces of her mind and the abundant energy of her body. Briefly, she held Silver Top's attention and then slipped off. He heard the musical echo of her voice in the kitchen.

He made a quick meal of it and rose to go. On the threshold of the room he heard the kitchen door open and he turned to see her silhouetted against the light; her whole body appeared to be rigid and she held one hand up to her eyes. Whatever was in them could not be seen and he left the

14

place and embarked upon the street, troubled of mind. The stable roustabout's cigarette tip glowed in the dark night. Here and there gleamed a light and down at the Halfway Resort, a piano jingled a honky-tonk tune. Men moved by him casually, speaking softly when they spoke at all. And again Silver Top made note of figures posted at odd places, eyeing him as he passed. The Halfway Resort drew him on.

"It's a place I shouldn't be goin' to," he reflected, stopping in front of it. "But I can't be turnin' my back like a yaller dog."

That was only half a reason and he knew it well enough. The truth was, he thirsted for light and cheer and the sound of men's voices. Solitude had claimed him too long and so, throwing caution aside, he opened the doors of the saloon and walked sedately to the bar. A brace of fingers extended toward the bartender served to supply him and he poured himself a conservative drink, holding it up against the light. Someone spoke at his elbow.

"It ain't fittin' Bad News should let a gent drink alone. Pass me a glass, Mike."

It was Ab Deering, smiling in a tight and covert manner. Silver Top waited until Deering had filled his glass, then raised his arm courteously. Deering threw out his immense chest.

"Here's to state lines, pardner, and may they make them closer together. Bad News takes you to the fold."

They drank. Deering smacked his lips and nodded toward the bottle. But Silver Top shook his head and reached for his money. Deering raised a hand. "It's on the house, amigo."

"You don't know me," said Silver Top with more than his usual bluntness.

"I do and I don't," replied Deering. "But I know a good man when I see one. I'm proud to have you enter my emporium. No questions asked, none answered. As for you, that rule on the wall don't apply. Yo're a guest of the shebang."

His short, heavy arm directed Silver Top's gaze to a crudely-lettered sign above the bar. Silver Top read it, chuckling.

15

THE LORD WILL PROVIDE. BUT HOW ABOUT THE GUY WHICH AIN'T GOING THAT WAY? MONEY ON THE BAR!

"Genius," approved Silver Top. He saw Deering's face assume a kind of proprietorship and the brittleness returned to his words. "I think you've got me wrong. Read yore cards again."

"I see a joker," was Deering's retort. The man moved off. Silver Top hooked his elbows into the bar and surveyed the room, which was rapidly growing more crowded. There was choice enough for every man's taste from faro to solitaire, and presently he made his way to a blackjack game and sat down. It was a fast pace the players set, but he laid small bets and was contented with winning and losing small pots. In fact he seemed to care nothing for the game itself, murmuring. "Hit," or "I'll play these," in a drawling, disinterested fashion. What he liked was the sound of men's voices, the pungent, acrid smell of the place and the light and warmth. Companionship, of a sort. Though from time to time when he raised his eyes and swept the circle he discovered that others were studying him closely and that he was, all unwi'ling, being cast as a member of a play which was even then going on in a silent, subtle fashion. Trouble was in the air; he felt it as distinctly as a draft of air on his back, and the physical effect on him was about the same. His nerves grew taut and his manner still more casual.

"He who lives by the sword shall die by the sword." Well, that was right. He had seen them strut along, proud of their temporal glory, then be snuffed out miserably at the hands of one a second faster on the draw. Always there was a man just a little faster than the one before. But how about the fellow who did not strut, who did not seek glory, and yet had the name of a fighter pinned on him? What about the fellow who hated gunplay and yet had to fight? Silver Top looked so grimly at his cards that the dealer said, "Pay, sixteen," and turned over his cards.

"Pay me," murmured Silver Top, disclosing two kings.

"You fooled me with that humble look," said the dealer. "It takes trainin' to do that."

Silver Top kicked back his chair and got up, strolling toward the door. The Halfway Resort was humming with voices and through the pall of smoke he saw men draped casually here and there; men who did nothing at all, but whose eyes were narrow and watchful. And he felt them boring into the small of his back as he went through the doors and into the street.

"A fine dish of trouble," he murmured. "Sodom and Gomorrah rolled into one. No wonder that Dixon hombre has got worry in his eyes. But what would anybody harm him for?"

The roustabout was slouched on the bench in front of the stable and when Silver Top sat down beside him his cigarette tip described an oval in the velvet shadows. "Mebbe you've seen aplenty to convince ya," said he.

"Folks have a habit of speaking in circles hereabouts," mused Silver Top. "No, that ain't it either. The idea seems to be to get somewhere without leavin' tracks."

"Words is fatal," observed the roustabout pessimistically, his voice sagging to a ridiculous whisper. "But I was alludin' to totin' a gun."

"Did a gun ever bring you anything, amigo?" asked Silver Top, his voice filling.

"It's a-kept me from shuckin' my sperrit a time or two."

"A man never knows when he's better off dead," said the gaunt newcomer. The roustabout, peering across the chasm of defeated hope and broken health, marveled that this man who walked so straight and looked so straight could put so much despair into his words.

"You better pack a few pounds of iron," he reiterated, doggedly. "They ain't a man in Bad News that could get insurance."

Silver Top plunked the direct question. "Why?" He knew better, of course, but he wanted to see how the roustabout would squirm around it. The roustabout surprised him with a few vehement words.

"I'm crazy to be wagglin' my tongue to a stranger. But I know a center fire man when I sees him. This town ain't no better'n a snake nest. It ain't. Put walls around it and you'd have a dang fine collection for a penitentiary. They's a few square citizens here—but they're walkin' soft with one eye cocked backwards. Same to you. You'll have to declare yoreself purty soon. They've got you marked, friend. They's been gents posted around that hotel ever since you landed here. Better get a gun."

"Thanks," said Silver Top. One hand fell lightly across the roustabout's shoulders and tarried a brief instant. It had all the effect of an accolade, and the roustabout gurgled something unintelligible. It had been a long, long time since anybody had treated him as a man.

"Mortality," murmured Silver Top, "is the lot of man. It's pretty hard to kill a fellow when you don't want to."

"It's plumb harder to be killed," retorted the roustabout.

"I ain't so shore of that," said Silver Top, each word falling slowly across the shadows. "No, I ain't so shore of that."

Something squat and black drew out of the shadows and stopped. The roustabout's breath seemed to catch in his throat. Ab Deering's blunt voice spat at them. "You boys oughtn't to sit in a draft. It's bad on the lungs. Stranger, I'd be plumb pleased to have a word with you in the rear of my establishment. Nothin' business-like. Jus' a social affair."

Silver Top rose and without comment followed Deering's bulky figure down the street. They ducked into an alley unbelievably black, turned a corner and struck a door. Yellow lamplight gushed out of an aperture and a latch clicked. Silver Top found himself in a little room back of the saloon. Overhead, feet stamped on the pine boards and from the bar came the rattle and clink of bottles. Life in the Halfway was at full flood. Deering poked his thumb at a chair and Silver Top sat down. Deering did likewise and thus they confronted each other, across the narrow space of a poker table.

"Drink?" asked Deering.

Silver Top shook his head, studying his man. The new-

18

comer appeared half asleep; everything about him was slack, easygoing. Yet behind his false front his brain revolved swiftly and every move of the squat and ugly saloon proprietor registered instantly within him. He was as cold as ice, this stranger, and strange currents began to feed his vision, the muscles of his arms and his fingertips.

"I got a gun here," began Deering, "which I'd like yore opinion on. It shoots straight, but I was wonderin' if it hefted jus' right in a man's hand. I'd be obliged for an expert opinion. Nothing unfriendly meant when I produce it."

It came from beneath the table, butt forward. Deering waited until Silver Top turned the palm of his hand upward, then dropped it therein. He watched the slim, artist's fingers slowly close around the grip and the index finger twine through the trigger guard. Nothing escaped the intent eyes of the saloon proprietor. Once he looked upward, and something like grim satisfaction registered on his swart face when he saw the changing light on Silver Top's countenance. The gun became a dull flash as it spun and came to rest again. Silver Top's thumb rubbed tentatively across the flange of the hammer and he lifted it ever so little from its bed.

"A right good weapon," he drawled at last.

Deering drew a breath and relaxed. "I thought you'd find it so. Well, take it with my compliments."

"I'm obliged, but no. I ain't got no need to shoot my meals any more. I buy 'em."

Deering waited until the gun rested idle on the table. Then his right arm shot across the intervening space with surprising deftness and ripped Silver Top's coat lapel back, revealing the vest. Silver Top hardly moved. Something like a grin flitted over his lean countenance.

"If yo're lookin' for a star I ain't that breed of horse, amigo. But if you wanted to know the brand of suspenders I wear, go ahead and look."

"I thought for a minute I was fooled," he acknowledged. "Usually I can read a gent first glance."

"There's plenty of readin' matter in me," confessed Silver Top in that same thin drawl, "but it's been sorter mutilated

19

beyond the power to decipher."

"No," contradicted Deering, leaning forward, "they's one thing plain about you. That's yore three-cornered eyes. It tells me ample. I ain't askin' nothin', understand? But we'll work fine together."

"Who are you?" said Silver Top, bluntly.

"Me?" Deering's fists closed and dropped on the table like lumps of iron. "I'm the law in Bad News! I've got enough power behind me to shave this town down to the grass roots. When I talk above a whisper they hear it on the far edge of the county. And they come on the jump! Understand? What lives and eats around these parts does so by my permission. See?"

"The duly constituted authority of the incorporation bein' demised?" said Silver Top, just above a whisper.

"I own the marshal," acknowledged Deering with a snarl of his thick lips. "I let the mayor, old man Dixon, play at his job jus' out of fun."

Silver Top drew a breath. "I'm thankin' you for the instructions. Now I'll hie me to the bunk."

"You ain't so dense but what you get what I'm drivin' at."

"Yo're shootin' sage hens with a cannon, friend. I don't need protection because I ain't holdin' up no stages or doin' any private killin'.'"

Deering's round face blackened; there was a yellow flash of his eyes. Half rising, he delivered his threat. "You'll play poker with me or you'll play a harp."

"I doubt if Saint Peter'd trust me with such a valuable musical instrument," averred Silver Top and calmly walked out through the door and down the dark alley. He heard a foot crunch behind him and the rapid exchange of soft words. In the street he rubbed his hands down the side of his coat and blotted the sweat from beneath his hat brim.

"There's the spider's den," he muttered. "And there's the spider. A-weavin' his web and waitin' for stray flies. So I'm to be one of his agents and do his dirty errands and perform his killin' and the like. Blamed if he didn't mean it as a compliment. It must be hard to get high class material in Bad News."

He saw the roustabout framed in the door, but he was in no humor to parley any more this night. Ducking into the hotel he saw Dixon and the waitress by the counter. They were both watching him as he passed up the stairs; watching him with that queer veiled look in their eyes. It struck him that they knew he had talked with Deering—that they understood what had been told him. They were trying to read his answer. He let himself into his room, took off his boots, and dropped onto the bed. It seemed he was like an animal in the zoo with people prodding him with sticks to see which way he'd move.

It was the old story over again. Men were forever seeing in him something he didn't have; giving him credit for abilities he didn't possess. Years back, or so it seemed, he had gone into his first quarrel and from that quarrel had sprung a legend that he was a dangerous man to deal with. It was the kind of legend that spread, and from it had come most of his trouble. Others had challenged his dexterity—and they had gone down. He hated to kill; he hated to be thought of as a killer. Yet they had made one of him. In self defense he walked like a killer and studied others in the killer's manner. Even kept his fingers supple and his nerves steady as a killer had to keep them.

Well, he had survived, but at night he saw those men he had sent down. Saw them just as his bullet struck them and they pitched forward. One by one they marched across the dark ceiling and toppled over. And he had spoken from his heart when he told the roustabout that he wasn't sure whether it was easier to live than to die. Dead men had no memories.

So he was fleeing from his old stamping ground and abandoning his friends, leaving behind his guns and every piece of gear that had the blood-scent to it. Trying to straighten a life that had been badly twisted by a legend. Now what was happening but the old story over again? Bad News had

21

looked at him, seen his lean grim face and his triangular eyes and they were calling him a dangerous man!

"I could run away," he muttered. "There ought to be some place in this man's world where I wouldn't have to buck all this." But he knew he was lying to himself. His pride wouldn't let him run away; the challenge had been laid down to him and if he left Bad News they would call him yellow. He could even see Dixon and the waitress looking at him with disapproval in their worried eyes.

Somebody passed in the hallway and brushed the knob of his door. Listening, he heard feet bear down on a loose board of the floor and finally slide away. Silver Top shrugged his shoulders. Presently he was asleep.

He moved about very little the next day. In fact, he never left the hotel porch; but he was aware that the invisible telegraph carried his every gesture down to the Halfway Resort. Deering sat next to him at supper, never saying a word. And that night there was again somebody patrolling the hall and touching the knob of his door.

"It'll bust pretty soon," he told himself. "After the heat comes the thunder. Well, I guess I've got to face it. I guess I've got to."

Still he made no move to arm himself. His reason told him to get a gun and all his impulses bade him sit still and hope that this droning, evil little town would mind its own business. Yet he knew, as the third day moved onward toward sunset, that the crisis was approaching rapidly. The years of training back of him had given him that sixth sense by which some men can feel the unseen machinery of destiny moving onward. Just little straws blown along in the wind—such as the fact that old man Dixon had opened his safe doors before supper to let a solitary horseman deposit a long, thick bundle. This person, Silver Top noted, packed two revolvers and a sawed-off shotgun; and at the supper table he sat with his back to the farthest wall and watched the men of the room with plainly hostile eyes. Silver Top made a note that Deering was absent, and after eating he went to the porch, his face settling and growing somber. Across the way the

22

roustabout was moving around at his chores and Silver Top checked the inclination to amble over and pass a few words. He never knew that the roustabout was praying he would sit still another brief hour.

For the roustabout could read signs, too. He had lived too long in Bad News not to know what it meant when Deering absented himself from Dixon's table; or when the marshal began to pull nervously at his long mustache and look sidewise over his shoulders. So the roustabout kept his counsel and tried to keep the fear from showing through his faded eyes. And when the black prairie shadows fell like a cloak across the flimsy street he let himself out of the stable's rear door, picked a cautious path through the littered back lots, and dropped like a plummet at the back entrance of the Halfway Resort.

They were already inside the dim and smoky room. The roustabout could see them through the window, and after tarrying a moment to whip his volatile courage to the surface he advanced to the window and raised his head. Deering was there, surrounded by three others, including the marshal; and Deering was giving out orders gruffly; too sure of himself to lower his voice. The roustabout heard all that he wanted to hear.

"He'll make some sort of play," Deering was saying. "I dunno what, but I'm bettin' he's here to pick up that payroll from the safe. Prob'bly had advance notice when it was comin' through."

"Supposin' that ain't his game?" queried the marshal.

"We'll pin the trick on him!" shot back Deering. "Anything to trump up a charge or two. Jus' for form's sake. He can't hold out on me. I'll show him who's boss. Bill, you cover this door. Nail him when he breaks out. Joe, it's up to you to ride herd on the messenger. Natcherilly he'll be listenin' for stray noises, so be careful. I'll take care of that safe. You know what I said about Dixon. Drink on it and mosey along."

The roustabout stepped back, retraced the path to the stable, and stopped in the comfortable security of the place, breathing hard. They meant to crucify Silver Top because he wouldn't bend his neck to Deering's yoke. Shoot him cold or manufacture evidence that he'd broken that safe and got the money from it. Oh, there was money there, all right. That messenger was taking it to the Roaring Nellie Mine southward. As for the messenger, he'd be killed cold. And Deering wasn't doing it because he needed an alibi for the law. Not especially; he was framing Silver Top out of pure spite.

"An' that white-haired fool ain't even got so much as a toothpick for a wee-pon," groaned the roustabout.

He had about reached the limit of his nerves. Even now the shadows began to bother him and he kept thinking he heard somebody moving in a rear stall. This wouldn't do at all, for the hardest chore was still before him. He had to warn Silver Top and the thought of it made him cold from head to foot. Him, an old broken-down workhorse have the gall to tell a better man what to do? Why, Silver Top was like to blast him off the earth with a few well-picked words. Nevertheless, it had to be done. The roustabout, remembering the manner in which Silver Top had fraternally rested an arm across his shoulders, went to a distant recess and found his gun. It wasn't much of a wee-pon for a fighter like Silver Top, he admitted humbly, but it had to do. It jus' had to do.

Again he left the stable, this time crawling in the opposite direction. At the street's end he crossed over and worked back to the hotel, coming up by the side of the porch. Silver Top was there alone, rocking gently in his chair. The roustabout raised himself, slipping the gun over the railing.

"Here, grab this, amigo. They got you boxed. Tonight. The works is downstairs in that safe—an' for Gawd's sake, don't walk out of yore door when you hear 'em come!"

He was gone, ducking against hotel wall and expecting to hear a bullet come crashing after him at any moment. He was playing a game beyond his limit and he well knew it. "If I ever git back to that stable alive I'll tend to my own fool business," he grunted. But apparently no one had seen him and he reached his haven out of breath and in an agony of suspense. There was a burst of gunplay down by the First Chance where two drunks were finishing an argument; but around the hotel it was as quiet as a grave. Silver Top's shadow was gone from the porch. The roustabout waited.

Silver Top had tucked the revolver into his pocket and after a few discreet minutes had risen and gone inside. Dixon was reading a week-old paper and Silver Top saw the man's eyes waver from the print and follow him as he climbed the stairs. Usually there was another man or so in the big front room; tonight it was bereft of company and Silver Top understood well enough why it was so. The invisible telegraph had warned Bad News to stay clear of that end of town. He reached his room and was about to go in when he heard the click of a latch and a single low, half-audible word. "Wait."

He turned to face the waitress. Standing near the head of the stairs, she was faintly outlined by the reflection of the light from the big room, and Silver Top felt again the impact of her somber eyes and the repressed energy of her straight, full-bosomed body. One hand was raised toward him. "Here is a key," she said. "It will fit your door."

"What would I be needin' with a key?"

"You have no guns, have you?"

He shook his head, nor did he accept the key. In fact, he didn't really think that she meant him to have it. There was something behind the offer—a warning to be on the alert, to take care of himself.

"I'm thankin' you," he muttered. "Folks seem to want to help me somehow."

She moved forward and just for an instant her arm brushed his coat sleeve. He thought she meant to whisper something, so close did her head come to his. The next moment she was gone, leaving in Silver Top's ears the rhythm of her step. He went into his room and lit the lamp, turning the flame very low. Quite methodically, he began to inspect his gun and with his bandanna to rub the working parts.

"Mortality," he drawled softly, "is shorely the lot of man. Ain't it funny how a fellow is always doin' something he don't want to? I'd as lief touch a snake as this cold iron. And here I am, back to my old tricks. Lord!"

There was a sound in the rear of the hallway—almost like the raising of a window. Down below Dixon was locking up for the night and in a little while he came above; Silver Top made a note of how the old man's feet dragged across the bare boards. "That is trouble pressin' him down." Bad News seemed unaccountably silent. Silver Top put the cartridges back in the revolver, blew out his light and took a station by the door.

"Dog eat dog," he murmured. "It's a meat-eatin' world and if a man don't like meat he's plumb out of luck. In a minute the play'll be up to me, I reckon."

He raised his arm to the half-opened transom and felt the air scouring through. A window or door was open along the hall and he knew there was someone stationed just outside—waiting for him to walk into a trap. He smiled grimly. Well, others had spread bait like this for him. If they wanted a fight, damn 'em, they would get it. The guns would blaze once more and the powder would sting his nostrils and he would see somebody belching out a word and toppling forward. Only this time it might be him. There was always somebody just a little faster on the draw, always a time when the luck turned.

Of a sudden the place was full of small sounds. The wind slapped against the window shades, boards snapped—and from downstairs came a sharp, definite click, as of a lock being forced. This was a night when Dixon and Dixon's roomers would do well to sleep soundly. Silver Top shook his head in pity for the messenger who had to go out and face this piece of trouble. As for himself, it didn't matter. But they were bold enough about it, below. Some of Deering's men, no doubt, and they knew Deering had the whole place buffaloed. Still, it seemed like unnecessary insult to walk so boldly across the floor.

Silver Top raised himself to his full height. A knob rattled and turned and hard upon it came a single explosion that jarred every board in the place. A man's voice, high and gurgling, emitted two or three terribly twisted words; then a body slid down with a double impact of knees and arms. Silver Top drew a breath; it was his play now if ever. He slid across the door and yanked it open, plastering himself to a corner. A purplish light flared in his very face and his ears rang with the pressure of the sharp report. Fair target. He fired once and knew that he had struck his man. There was a grunt, a suspiring breath, and again the jarring of the pine boards. Silver Top slid through the door and ducked to his knees. He sought and found the other fellow's gun, raised up and ran toward the head of the stairs.

Dixon had left a lamp on the counter, the flame turned well down. But there was a face framed by the saffron glow—a face swart and evil. It was Deering himself—Deering doing his own dirty work, for some strange reason. And Deering stared upward at the invisible Silver Top and growled impatiently. "Well, boys, what's happened?" Another figure slid through from the porch, muttering, ". . . hell of a lot of noise. They's apt to be some shootin' from the street in a minute."

"Who's there?" challenged Deering.

The street reverberated with a swift, vicious fusillade. Men began to shout and Silver Top heard Dixon's voice, out somewhere on the second-story porch, yelling, "Plaster that fella goin' into the shadows! We got 'em runnin'!" The man beside Deering whirled and ducked out of the place, leaving the barrel-chested one alone. The game was going awry; resistance had surprised him and the unexpected exchange of bullets in the street left him without the aid of his henchmen. Still he remained rooted, his heavy voice booming. "Who the devil's up there?"

It was a bull-headed thing to do and Silver Top had a flash of admiration for the man. He came down the steps three at a time. "I told you once, amigo, I didn't need yore protection."

"The white head, huh?" snarled Deering. "Well, why didn't you start goin'?"

"I'll give you an even draw, brother."

Deering stepped back a pace and with a single gesture turned up the wick of the lamp. The yellow light glowed upon them both; Deering's heavy jaws were slowly working and his eyes were like two brilliant beads framed in uneven jet stone. Silver Top's face was drawn and bleak and his long artist's fingers were holding both guns downward a full arm's length. "Draw, mister. It's fifty-fifty with me."

"No favors asked, you addle-headed fool!" bellowed Deering. "An' I took you for a first-class killer! What's this—Sunday School?"

Silver Top watched one bulky hand fall, hang suspended, and rise again. Nor did he bring up his own guns until Deering's weapon seemed full upon him. The short and ugly one already was grinning at his victory and the grin was still on his face when Silver Top fired. Deering never saw the other's gun come up and his stubborn pride seemed to refuse to admit that he had been hit. But strength oozed out of him and pride alone would not hold him. Twisting about, he fell and his last, guttural words were: "Who in hell are you, amigo?"

Silver Top seemed to be listening to something else. The gaunt face lost every measure of its grimness. "Mortality," he sighed. "It's the lot of man." He seemed to turn angry. "Damn you and yore kind! Why can't you let a gent live peaceably with his conscience? I'm Joe Lane of Montana. Now turn over and die!" His arms came up and both guns went through the air, smashing against the counter. "I hope I never set eyes on a gun again!"

Thus he stood, his blue eyes losing their flame and his long body bent as if in utter exhaustion, when Dixon came down and there was a sudden inrush of men from the street. Dixon carried a sawed-off shotgun in his hand and his wrinkled old face was wreathed in victory. "You got him, Silver Top! God bless you, man! He never figgered we could make a last stand. Well, we did. I lined up five-six boys on the quiet and we crimped him. This town is going to go to the laundry. I knew blamed well you'd choose right."

"Choose which?" asked Silver Top.

"Deering's side or the law's side. Gents, the evening's very young. We ain't done half what we should. They's twenty men what need to be run off or shot down. They'll make no hell-hole of this place!"

The talk swirled around Silver Top. He raised his eyes and swung them from side to side, suddenly finding the waitress halfway up the stairs. The light was full upon her, the shadows dispelled. And she was looking at him as he had never seen a woman look before. There was a tension to her whole vigorous body and a flame of color in her cheeks. Silver Top held her glance but an instant and turned away, shamed at himself.

Dixon shook his fists at the street and looked at Silver Top. "I'm mayor here and my word goes from now on until a duly constituted election. I'm making you marshal pro tem. Come on."

"Nope," said Silver Top, "I've done enough for one night."

"Movin' on?" queried Dixon, plainly disappointed.

Silver Top looked back at the girl and seemed to find his answer. "No, I guess I'm stayin' awhile." Then he squared his shoulders. "Oh, hell, this town's been good to me. I'll pay my debt." And he walked over and retrieved his guns. He was the last one out of the place and on the threshold he swung about, to find the girl smiling at him.

In the street he found the roustabout hobbling behind the posse, an old buffalo gun cradled in his arms. He saw Silver Top and raised an incredulous voice. "I nev' expected to live to see this day."

"It's better to live than to die," said Silver Top. "It shorely is."

GRASSHOPPER DANCE

Here and there on the prairie's flatness a few houses made blurred shapes beneath a brass-colored atmosphere that got thicker and thicker on the horizon, like the sullen boil-up of fire smoke. Sitting on the load of wood, Dan Gay saw that only he and his horses ventured abroad in the blistered loneliness of the day. There was no heat like this heat. It sucked the moisture out of his bones and burned against his skin in the way acid burns.

It was a relief to see Ivan Goerisch's house two hundred yards ahead. Dan Gay slanted his hat against the lower strike of the sun and stepped down to the tongue, never trying to push his horses faster. When they drew abreast of the house he said "Whoa," gently and dropped to the dirt. There was trouble here, and he knew at once what the trouble was; for Ivan Goerisch stood at the well in the middle of the yard, holding rope and bucket in his great arms. He looked up to the approaching Dan Gay. "Dry," he said. "I been afraid of that."

Sweat streaked down his face; it plastered his shirt against the massive arch of his chest. He was a huge young man, with power enough in his arms to wrestle a horse, but his eyes were mild blue and his cheeks pink as a girl's cheeks, and his voice was small and shy. "Well, you're pretty thirsty. I got a little in the bucket on the porch."

Dan Gay went to the porch and took enough water to dampen his throat. The two of them sat in the false shade a short time while Dan Gay built himself a smoke. He felt no extra heat from the lighted match when he touched it to his cigarette. "So I guess it's really warm."

"Dan," said Ivan Goerisch, showing trouble in his eyes, "it is another bad year. How long can a man hang on?"

"Long as there's seed for another year. You're going to the dance tomorrow?"

The increased pink of Ivan's cheeks betrayed him and he could not meet Dan Gay's glance. "Listen. You're going by that way. You tell her I got no heart for dancin'."

Dan Gay rose and strolled back to his wagon, the big German tramping behind, trying to express himself. "What have I got to offer a woman? I should not be serious with Clara Brecht."

Dan Gay swung up to the wagon. A broken pane of glass in the yard burned like fire. Sand lay in rippled rows against the side of the barn and the glare of the day pressed against his eyeballs. He grinned at Ivan Goerisch. "I'll say you'll be coming by, around eight. Tch—Fanny, Duke!"

He adjusted the straw-stack seat and considered this smoky land with a deep, personal resentment. Dry winter and dry spring had turned into this; and all things lay burned and eroded and ruined beneath the incredible sun. Goerisch's eighty acres of wheat made a stunted stand, the grain tops already turned black, and elsewhere as here men stood on the edge of their fields and saw disaster. He pulled the brim of his hat down, and pulled his shoulders forward, as though to present a lesser target to the sun. One more mile brought him to Emero Dulaney's place and here he went in with a bucket and drew water for his horses. Emero came from the house, tall and faded and made gaunt by his long labor. His hair had one pure streak of white running through it. His eyes were almost green against the leather blackness of his skin. He had a soft, exhausted voice.

"You suppose hell could be as hot as this?"

"The rain will come."

"Nothing will be saved."

"Seed for next year, maybe," said Dan Gay.

"I've had too many years of it."

A woman's insistent, high-toned voice came from the house. "Dulaney, I want you."

Dulaney's eyes changed. He said softly: "She's worse."

Dan Gay called: "Bring your fiddle tomorrow night."

"Sure, sure," said Dulaney and went into the house, into the stifling twilight of a room whose shades had been drawn. A woman walked endlessly along the room, her face pale and odd. Dulaney murmured gently, "It was Dan Gay, hauling wood to Dry Ford," and touched and stopped her. He took her hands and led her to a chair and sat opposite, in another chair. He kept his voice at a steady and soothing tone. "He's a fine young fellow. A fine young fellow, and a hard worker. The rain's coming, Anna, and it will be nice after a while."

"Trouble will come to him, Dulaney."

"Trouble," he said, "comes to us all. But we can bear it. We can bear it, Anna. It will be cooler, it will be greener. There is nothing to fear." His rough palm moved across her hands and his talk softly fought the silence that frightened her so.

An hour's slow march brought Dan Gay to the Brecht ranch lying on the rim of Sawyer's coulee. He pulled in again and waited for Clara Brecht to come out to the road. She walked with a long, vigorous swing. She was a big girl, almost as tall as Dan Gay, and it took a man like Ivan Goerisch to put her in proportion. Pleasant and pretty, she looked up at Dan Gay with a kind of eagerness.

"He'll be by tomorrow about eight," said Gay, and grinned.

Clara Brecht said: "He is so quiet for a man."

Dan Gay said: "Never mind, Clara. I'm helpin' out on this and I've got words enough for both of us." And then they were both smiling, both aware of the humor here. He said, "Tch—Fanny, Duke!"

Another mile on, he came to his own fields lying gray and blistered on either side of a creek that long ago had ceased to hold water. One thing alone remained green—that was the garden patch behind the long sod house—kept so by the tedious hours of watering he had put upon it. Elsewhere nothing hopeful met the scanning of his eyes. He turned and put the wagon in motion, disappointment scouring brutally through him. He pulled at his hat again and his mouth grew thinly long and all his features began to resist this day's savageness. Anger lifted his temper and silently he swore at the sun; but none of this came out because he would not let it. Beyond his ranch the road turned gently into Dry Ford, which was a town made up of a few houses and a store set at the joining corners of four homesteads. In front of Jeff McTeague's store he stopped and stood up on his load, and began to drop cordwood in a forming row, his body swaying automatically, without waste of motion, without extra expense of energy.

The sun was a blurred explosion of light in the low west. After it dropped, a kind of peace began to creep across the land and the air turned blue and the upward rising heat of the soil increased the pungent odors of dust and parched wood.

Across the road John Flora's nine towheaded girl children played in the dust, their clothes hanging without shape to nervous, sun-blackened bodies. Flora and his wife were inside the house, talking in the loud tone of all homesteaders. A woman said, from the store porch:

"When will you be through, Dan?"

Dan Gay stood still on the wagon, his legs straddling the wood. He said, "Not long," and looked at Persis McTeague, the acute awareness of her presence hurting him more than this hard day. She was twenty-two, with the full freshness of womanhood stirring all the supple lines of her body. Her hair had a gloss-black shine in the subdued atmosphere and her lips were sober and curved and waiting. In a land that so wickedly drew vitality out of people, this girl remained alive, prompted by inner life, governed by some deep rhythm.

He said briefly, "It won't be long," and bent to his work again.

She remained a moment, one arm curved against a porch post, a quicker breathing swaying and reforming the round, robust lines of her shoulders as she watched him. His silhouette was clean and sharp against the western light. The muscles of his arms swelled the damp cotton shirt when he lifted and flung down the cordwood; his bronze features remained steady. There was a blackness about this man, a ruggedness and something dangerously stubborn. Observing the clocklike sway of his body, she suddenly lowered her eyes and was ashamed of the faint immodesty of her thinking. She went into the store and on back to the living quarters behind.

Full twilight curled through Dry Ford and Mrs. Flora stood in the dark doorway of her house and sent a long, full call after her children. "Come in to supper!" The edge of the heat was gone, but the thick and smoky smell of the land remained. Dan Gay finished unloading. He unhitched the team and drove it to water; and later unharnessed and stalled the horses in Jeff McTeague's barn. He washed at the well pump, throwing water on the back of his neck, cupping it in his hands and pushing his face into its coolness. Afterward he went through the kitchen to the lamplit dining room. They sat up to the table when he came—McTeague and McTeague's wife and Persis, and Jack Curran, who was a young man visiting from Chicago.

This Jack Curran had a good face and a laughing way. His clothes were Eastern—of a sort Dan Gay had almost forgotten in his five prairie years; and he wore them with ease. There was no resentment in Dan Gay as he listened to Curran talking, only a feeling deeper than regret.

Curran said, in his casual, cheerful manner: "Back home now, I should be taking a swim in the lake."

Jeff McTeague said: "You'll soon be out of this dry country, Jack."

"I have not minded it here," Curran murmured and looked across at Persis McTeague with his hope plain enough. It was, Dan Gay understood, the reason for Curran's

34

visit. He was tired, that feeling going deeper into his bones. Dust and heat had lighted a fire inside his eyelids and he drank his water with a suppressed greediness. Jeff McTeague studied him with a Scotchman's remote, shrewd interest.

"Tomorrow will be as hot. You'd better let the wood-hauling alone for a few days."

Jack Curran said: "When did it rain last in this country?"

"April," said Jeff McTeague. "April fifteenth." He put his hand up to a small white chin-beard and held it there; and his attention divided between the two young men—and passed to his daughter. What he saw there he put in the back of his head.

Jack Curran said: "I admire you people—and I pity you. It is hard for me to understand why you stay."

Dan Gay moved his shoulders faintly. "Long as there's seed left for spring I guess we'll stick. Dulaney's woman is worse than she has been, poor soul."

Jack Curran said: "Dulaney's woman?"

Dan Gay stared at his plate. "She lost a baby three years ago. It changed her."

"Mad," Jeff McTeague stated.

"No," contradicted Dan Gay. "Not mad. Just changed."

There was sound of travel out on the road, and someone came into the store. Night had released the roundabout settlers. Jeff McTeague got up and went forward to wait upon his customer. Mrs. McTeague, as silent as her husband, turned back to the kitchen. Persis followed and got the coffeepot and filled the two men's cups. She put the pot on the table mat and sat down again. She sought Dan Gay's eyes with an interest that faintly changed the color of her face. He was relaxed in his chair, staring at the table, some bold thought pulling a dark mask across his forehead. Jack Curran said gently, "Persis," and brought her glance to him. He was smiling out his hope to her.

She had known him since Iowa childhood, and she knew him well. But there was still an unreality here that had the quality of a dream about it. The gift was hers, for a smile and a nod of her head—release from this land's monotony

35

and cruel ways, from the deep loneliness that hurt so much. Looking through the door Jack Curran held open, she saw a world that was full of luxury. In that world was light and pleasure—and escape from the swift age that came to women here.

She could not help her eyes. They turned again to Dan Gay. She knew then he had seen the unworded offer cross the table from Curran. He understood. Faint fear touched her. She said, "Dan."

Sudden brawling sounded out on the road. Men's voices lifted through the store, ungentle and wicked, and the stage from Elyria boomed across the plank bridge and stopped with a dry howling of brakes. The voices rose louder. Dan Gay rose and went immediately into the store. Jeff Mc-Teague looked up from his chore at the dry-goods counter. He said dryly: "The Randolph boys are drunk again." Dan Gay continued on to the porch and stood there at one end, half surrounded by a gathering group of homesteaders. Store lights flashed through the door and made a yellow stripe across the porch; behind that yellow stripe stood the two bully Randolph boys, swaying, enjoying the staid silence they had created among the little group of homesteaders. This was their way—to get drunk and seek trouble. Scanning them darkly, Dan Gay saw that the larger brother, Ben, carried a gun on his hip.

Ben Randolph said casually: "What're you hidin' for, Dan?"

The smells of the store were wafted along the porch—the mingling aroma of soap and leather and coffee and dry goods. A man came down the road swinging a lantern. Somewhere, precious water dripped into a trough. The crowd drifted quietly, reforming against the store wall, leaving Dan Gay alone. The driver of the Elyria stage sat up on his seat and delayed departure, looking on with an alert interest.

"Talk up to me," suggested Ben Randolph and walked

36

forward. He was within arm's reach. He lifted one big hand, whereupon his brother came up behind him, flat-footed and grinning. Dan Gay's body shifted in the semi-dark. His voice ran low: "I heard you're looking for somebody to lick."

Ben Randolph was laughing. He said, "Artie, this man's scared," and reached out and caught Dan Gay by the shirt. They were two bulky shapes—and then those shapes became a single shadow wheeling across the porch. Dan Gay's arms lifted and lowered and echoes squashed against the quiet and Ben Randolph was yelling out his unexpected hurt. His brother Artie wheeled and reached for Dan Gay and was caught in one spinning turn that threw him off the high porch, down under the feet of the stage horses. They were at the end of the porch. Dan Gay's fist reached Ben Randolph on the temple. Ben went down the steps in a crashing sprawl, out into the dim dust. He was on his feet, but Dan Gay rushed him without delay and dropped him again, and reached and got the man's gun and flung it far away.

Artie Randolph fought his way clear of the stage, crying: "I'm comin', Ben!" But John Flora, walking over the road's soundless dust, reached forward with his long arms and seized Artie Randolph with a grip that held him still. Lin Getchell turned out of McTeague's barn, coming unhurriedly on; and McTeague and Curran showed on the store's porch. When Ben Randolph rose to his feet again, all these men were here, with the other homesteaders.

Dan Gay said: "What'll it be, Ben?"

Artie grumbled at John Flora, "Let go." John Flora unwrapped his long arms and hovered over Artie Randolph darkly. Ben Randolph pushed the fingers of one hand across his lips. He stared at Dan Gay and at these others, his eyes showing the quick, hot way of his mind. He moved his shoulders together. "Come on, Artie," he called and turned from the scene to the horses waiting nearby. Both he and his brother were mounted and turning out of Dry Ford when

37

he made a half-turn in the saddle, crying: "Tomorrow's another night—and we'll see!" Afterward the two of them raced away.

Dan Gay turned and noticed the driver staring down from the stage box. He lifted his arm at the man. "You've had your fun. What're you waiting for?" He went past the store, tasting blood in his mouth. He cut over the road and turned the corner of Flora's house, aiming for his own place a mile away. There was a red moon shining down upon the earth, flushing a crimson shadow against the side of Flora's house. Persis McTeague stood there, a pale, still plaque against the boards.

"Dan."

He wheeled and stopped, his feet braced apart. "Persis," he said, "don't bother me."

"Are you hurt?"

He said irritably: "No."

Her body swayed against the wall. She didn't speak, but her face was clear to him, curious and dreaming and unhappy. He went toward her and saw that she didn't give ground. Her chin lifted as he came on and there was a shining in her eyes. Her breathing ran small and swift. A faint perfume in her hair cut through the thick odors of this full night. He didn't touch her. He stood that way a long time and presently swung off. He said, with some effort: "Dulaney's woman is changed and Mrs. Flora is old and wrinkled before her time. They were young and pretty once. That's what this country does to a woman. Why make Jack Curran wait so long?"

At three-thirty in the morning, when he reached Dry Ford to hitch his team, a wind rose up from the southern darkness, small and steady. At six, returning with his first load of wood, the sun laid its harsh flame across the low horizon and heat smoke had begun to filter in. But there was an odd feeling here, something shadowy and sinister rising from the south with the wind. Not quite up to Ivan Goerisch's place,

38

Dan Gay stopped his team. It was a waste of precious time, yet the insistence of his curiosity impelled him to turn and watch the yonder sky. Off there a moving cloud swelled higher and higher and came on, its ragged edges reaching forward and closing out the light of day, throwing grayness along the earth. As far as he might look, to east and west, there was no break, the cloud was that thick and that continuous.

Dan Gay crouched on the wood, his shoulders pushed forward. He had lighted a cigarette, but he held it between his fingers while his face turned thoroughly smooth and his half-closed eyes flashed out the bright light of his rousing attention. One edge of the cloud poured across the low sun and a kind of unnatural twilight dropped upon the earth. The horses swayed nervously against the wagon tongue; he had to check them with the reins. He saw Ivan Goerisch run from the house, throw one look at the sky and race toward the barn. There had been stillness in the land but now a low, dry rustle reached on from that thickening substance in the air—and Dan Gay whirled around on the wood and put his horses in motion. All his forebodings stood realized. Wind-borne and wind-controlled, a grasshopper horde swarmed through the air.

He had not quite reached Goerisch's when the edge of that living darkness slanted down upon the road and struck like leaden hail. The team yawed from the ruts. He bent the brim of his hat, but nothing could keep the boiling current of grasshoppers from striking against his face, the sharpness of their bodies scratching like needles. There was a sound like that of hail around him and all his clothes were alive with them as they lodged and stuck. He swung his bandanna around and lifted it over his nose and saw, in the unreal twilight, the flittering millions crowd and choke the air. It was at once hard to breathe.

He looked upon Ivan Goerisch's field with a stunned wonder. This wheat had ceased to be wheat. Each stem was a swollen column of grasshoppers and the whole patch slowly swayed in a kind of terrible motion; and there rose from it the sibilant sound of all those countless bodies striking together and all those hungry jaws stripping wheat head and wheat stalk.

Dan Gay went on down a road carpeted two inches deep with grasshoppers. At Dulaney's place they had lighted a fire and were raking grasshoppers into it and Dulaney's woman stood in her garden patch and beat pans together. Dulaney shouted at him, but Dan Gay only shook his bowed head and pressed on. When he reached his own place he left the horses standing hitched to the load and walked in long strides to the edge of his wheat field.

He had nourished a small hope that he might save part of a sun-scorched crop for seedtime. As soon as his eyes scanned the field that hope died. Looking on with a depthless discouragement, he saw his field slowly melt beneath the dull slate-and-copper-colored mass. He thought then of his garden and swung back. He got a rake from the back of the house and went along the garden rows. He raked the hoppers into piles and trod on the piles. They didn't rise and fly away. The blindness of their hunger and the weight of their incredible numbers trapped them. He turned from one row to another and found the first row to be thicker than before. He went up the second row, working fast. But they kept falling out of the sky, on his shoulders and arms, on down into the garden. It was like raking up water. At the end of the second row he looked around him and quit trying.

He threw the rake down, went back to the wagon and drove through the mealy, living storm into Dry Ford. There were some homesteaders standing solemnly on the store porch. He looked at them, but he didn't speak and they didn't speak. He backed the wagon against the woodpile and began to unload, his body lifting and swinging automatically, mechanically.

Other people came driving into Dry Ford. Ivan Goerisch came, riding his white plow horse bareback. Dulaney and his wife came in, Dulaney holding to his wife as he got out of

40

the buggy and still holding to her as they went into the store. Mrs. Flora walked across the road. She was crying and the effort made her face red and homely. One of the men struck his hand into his beard and stared at the hopper that he had crushed.

Dan Gay finished unloading and went around to the back of the store; he got himself a drink at the pump and stood there a moment, supporting his weight against the house wall. All of Jeff McTeague's wheat and corn—four hundred acres of it, stretching east toward a hidden sun—was down. Looking into a sky turned semisolid, he thought he saw clearness beyond the pall, but he wasn't sure. He went through the kitchen and dining room into the store. The homesteaders had gathered there; they were silent in this gloomy refuge. Breathing rose and fell with labor, and all their faces, as he saw them, were drawn and defeated. Persis McTeague was in a corner. Her eyes were waiting for him. They met his attention—and held it.

Ivan Goerisch opened his mouth and the heavy breathing momentarily stopped. "It is bad," he said quietly, "for the land to treat a man like this."

Dan Gay saw Jeff McTeague's bright and ironic glance touch the man. There was a remote and weighing speculation on the storekeeper's face. Over near Persis the young man from Chicago stood without much expression; listening and not smiling and plainly puzzled by the land and its people. Dulaney's woman swayed back and forth in the rocker.

An old German from the corner of the district said: "We are now ruined. There is nothing left. Nothing. This winter we go hungry."

Dan Gay bowed over his pipe, listening for honest anger in the German's voice and hearing only helplessness. He lighted his pipe and the flare of the match brought all those heavy, dispirited eyes around to him. He said:

"I remember how this country looked when I came here five years ago. No land in the world is any pleasanter than this land was then."

The stillness was deep. They were listening. The big German said: "It was then. It is not now."

Dan Gay stared at the German, so patient and so somber. Dulaney's woman called loudly, "Trouble will come again."

"No," said Dan Gay. There was something he wanted to tell them, but it would not shape up in his mind. "No," he repeated, gently insistent. "We're wiped out. Nothing more can happen to us. We can quit worryin'. We can start over—with nothing more to lose. You see?"

It wasn't any good. Brown inexpressiveness lay still and deep on all their faces. They had been whipped and there wasn't any fight left in them. There wasn't any hope left in them. He considered this, knowing he had nothing more to say, feeling beaten himself, yet stubborn and still willing to fight. And at this point he remembered the Randolph boys.

"Dulaney," he said, "don't forget to bring your fiddle to the dance tonight," and turned out.

McTeague's sharp voice caught him. "Where you going?"

"Back for another load. I don't figure the grasshoppers ate up the cordwood." He went back to his wagon, his head tipped against the falling hoppers.

At eight o'clock he walked down the road to Dry Ford in his blue serge suit and white shirt, feeling the unaccustomed stiffness of these clothes keenly, his shoes sinking soundlessly into the deep yellow dust. The wind had died and the air was clear, with a round moon throwing its stained light across a ruined land. Now and then the rasp of hoppers came to him from where they lay heavy and becalmed and half a yard deep in the ditches, in every furrow and coulee; where they would remain until another wind lifted them and carried them away. Over the quiet air he heard Herb Lazinka's guitar and the fiddle of Emero Dulaney carrying a waltz tune in Jeff McTeague's store.

Horses and rigs lay banked along the wide road running through the settlement and men stood in the soft shadows of the evening, their voices heavy and short with discouragement, with a low anger that could find no outlet.

He saw Persis McTeague come to the store's doorway and he went directly to her. Her face lifted and she smiled faintly at him and grew sober, as though afraid of what he might say. But a slow flame burned up its recklessness in him and he drew her back into the room and took her arm for the waltz.

McTeague had moved his center counter aside, and this made the dance floor. Homesteaders moved in and out of the doorway, and women sat in the corners, and a baby kept crying with a wound-up regularity. Ivan Goerisch went around the floor with Clara Brecht, casting his vast shadows before him, his pink cheeks constrained with the labor of dancing. But otherwise the hand of disaster lay over these people. It held them down; it even dragged at the music.

Persis said: "They've been whipped, Dan. So badly whipped."

He said: "Why do you stay here, Persis?"

She stepped back from him and her eyes were round and angry. "You are a fool, Dan. You—"

A man ran along the porch and put his head into the room. "Watch out. It's the Randolph boys." The sound of fast-traveling horses came quick and rough-paced along the night and Dan Gay, turning at once out of the store's room, heard Ben Randolph's long, loud crying: "Hey, Dan! Hey!" There were, Dan Gay saw, about a dozen wild young fellows from Grass Flats in this party. They came up at a gallop and hauled in by the porch, the silver dust rising all around; and then they were massed in the street, with Ben Randolph saying in his ragged, insolent voice, "Hey, Dan. I said we'd see, didn't I? Sure. Now we'll see."

Ivan Goerisch came out of the store. He said, "What is this?" and looked at the Randolph crowd with his blond head thrown back. Other men were coming around Dan Gay and Ivan, and Dan Gay could feel something here, something rising in these stolid and patient homesteaders who had taken so much punishment this day, something as definite as cool wind on his cheeks. Looking back, he saw Ivan Goerisch's blue eyes shining, and then he stepped down from the porch. Ben Randolph said, softly: "That's nice," and came on at a run. He reached Dan Gay's chest with his big fist, knocking Dan Gay backward. Dan felt Ivan Goerisch's big hand steady him and throw him forward into Randolph; and then Dan had Randolph around the chest, throwing him backward, and Ivan Goerisch had rushed toward the Grass Flats crowd, and the other homesteaders were running in, and voices began to pitch up, wild and pleased and passionate, and short, dull echoes rose as fist met flesh.

Dan Gay got his arms loose and hit Ben Randolph above the eyes. He drove against Randolph, carrying the man through this wild-turning crowd, hitting him and throwing him off his feet. Somebody ran out of the confusion and clipped Dan Gay on the back of the head and dropped him into the boiling dust. Dan Gay's brain roared and light burst brightly behind his eyeballs. He lay on one elbow, weakly pushing his other hand up to fend away legs and knees and lifted boots turning around him. He had lost Ben Randolph. Down in this melee, he saw nothing for a moment and had no time for anything except keeping himself from being trampled deeper into the dust. This was a hard, fast fight and the going was pretty savage. Somebody fell directly across him, bitterly swearing, and clawed up to the surface again. Dan Gay felt his head clearing and got up and was carried along between two pairs of battling men. Suddenly he saw Ben Randolph run at the broad back of Ivan Goerisch and make one huge jump onto the big man's shoulders. Dan Gay went on through the crush at a fast gait and seized Ben Randolph's legs, dragging him free. Ben Randolph yelled, "Let go—let go!" He had his face in the dust and his hands, working fast, couldn't keep him off the ground. Dan Gay dragged him unrelentingly through a crowd that had begun to break up. John Flora howled, "Run, damn your hides, run!" The Grass Flats crowd drifted backward, hard-breathing and badly used. Ivan Goerisch rammed through them and his voice was easy and soft, even while his big fists reached after them. Dan Gay threw Ben Randolph's legs free and watched the man crawl along the earth, half strangled by dust. Shadows streamed toward the near-by horses; shadows went up to the saddles. Artie Randolph yelled, "Ben, Ben," and found his brother and helped him to his feet. All this took a short moment and afterward the Grass Flats boys went racing down the road, leaving their deep-called defiance behind.

Dan Gay stood back from the grouped homesteaders, conscious of his own bruises; yet he listened to these men with a long care. They were silent for a little while, as though shaking themselves together. He saw Ivan Goerisch's great shape swing around and he saw the blond head tip and rise. Ivan said, "Dan—now that was some fun, hey?" And suddenly his laughter spilled into the quietness of Dry Ford, and then all these men were walking back to McTeague's store and Dan Gay, following, could see the pleased look on their brown cheeks; he could see the cracking of that starved, desperate hopelessness.

At once the fiddle and guitar swung into a fast tune and homesteaders were going into McTeague's eagerly. Coming up to the porch, Dan Gay found Persis waiting.

She said: "What are you laughing about?"

He hadn't realized he was until then. There was an ease in him, a coolness and a sense of well-being, as though trouble had never come. He looked at her, smiling. "Persis, it can never be so bad that we can't laugh."

Her eyes were watching him with a serious, intent regard, and he saw that she was puzzled. He said, "Well, we've all been licked for so long that we forgot what a good fight was like. So we had it and now everybody's cheerful again. Persis—"

She looked behind her and saw Jack Curran in the doorway. Yet she felt for the Easterner only a kind of vague sorrow, a sweet pity, and soon dismissed him from her mind. For Dan Gay held her shoulders and the long waiting was over, and inside the music got stronger and faster and people were calling.

RODEO

This third day of July began to lose its burning brightness, its breathless heat. A shapelessly red sun sank behind the western spur of the Tugwash Hills, flushing the opposite eastern spur with a last bannered and spangled radiance. At once the southern reaches of Absalom Valley, all afternoon hidden by the prairie's copper haze, began to rise through a clearer air. Partial quiet came to the talkative crowd, and into this quiet pitched the announcer's spaced-out words. "Last ride. Bob Kingman up on Captain Jack." Over on the mourners' bench those who already had ridden showed a greater interest and Howard Harpster's bronze call floated the width of the field. "Give him a play, Bob!" Colonel Henry Isom of Running US backed his pony to a corner of the arena for a better view of the performance; the other two judges likewise shifted.

Bob Kingman lifted his loose frame across the top of the chute and seated himself gently in the saddle. Captain Jack, nine hundred satin-black pounds of energy, trembled a little and his ears went flat. Seeing that, Bob Kingman's long mouth formed a tight grin. He kicked his feet securely into the stirrups, he rubbed his palms along his thighs. The man guarding the chute gate looked through an interstice and warned him casually, quietly: "Watch the third jump, Bob. He's got the damndest twist—" Kingman wrapped the hackamore rope twice around one hand and brought up the slack. For a lengthening interval he stared straight into the fading brightness of the arena, listening to the called advice, to the swelling volume of encouragement from the stands. Those people—friends and dwellers in this isolated little valley—wanted him to make the ride; he could feel that. The grin faded, his fibers were touched by sudden coolness, the preliminary nervousness died out of him. His free arm rose signalling to the sky. "All right, Bill, let 'er flicker."

The gate opened. Captain Jack, who was old at this business and who loved these battles, stiffened throughout. Kingman felt power surge into the brute like the turn-on of steam. Captain Jack swelled, his head dropped to his knees and he went out of the cramping chute in one high parabolic leap that snapped Kingman backward in the leather. Captain Jack's procedure was always the same—to pull his rider off balance, to stun him and to dump him. He came down with a terrific, stiff-legged smash and rose onward to another straining plunge. Kingman thought, "He explodes on the third one," and met the next assault loosely, muscles relaxed. Captain Jack grunted when he struck and the heavy shock ran up through flesh and leather and sledged Kingman at the base of the neck. Captain Jack ceased his forward rush and rose quivering on his two hind feet, and Kingman sighted the sky between the horse's pointed ears; then he was down in the dense dust, nursing his fine-drawn sense of balance while Captain Jack exploded into a furious fore-and-aft bucking. Meeting those detonating impacts, body whipped by each lunge and wrench, Kingman automatically scratched neck and withers. His hat fell, his hand remained aloft. There was a slight smell of blood in his nostrils and the arena's crisply outlined edges began to blur before him; women's white dresses made square patches against a massed background. Into his deep preoccupation the roar of the crowd broke only faintly and the report of Colonel Isom's gun not at all; but the pick-up men galloped forward from the rear and pinned Captain Jack between them. Kingman awkwardly slid across the rump of the left pick-up man's horse and dropped to the ground. There was an inevitable moment of reaction in which he walked aimlessly across the field in a straddling, bouncing manner. Then all things focused for him and he turned against the mourners' bench, chuckling.

"Was it a ride?"

The sorrel giant who was Howard Harpster said approvingly: "You'll qualify for tomorrow. Didn't doubt it, did you?"

Little Lou Pujo, sitting slightly apart from the other half-dozen contestants, put in his dry and somewhat hesitant word. "Good ride, Kingman."

"Thanks."

"Isom gave you a long one," observed Howard Harpster.

"The colonel," mused Kingman, "never favors his own hands."

"And never will," cut in another voice that was heavy and grudging. Howard Harpster had opened his mouth to speak, but he closed it and thrust an odd look at Kingman; a deliberate silence came to the group. Kingman, turning toward the other end of the bench, said, "Just so, LeTest," impassively. That was all, but his eyes remained on this LeTest, who was foreman of Running US and therefore his immediate boss. LeTest was standing. His thick legs—good bronc-rider's legs—ran straight down from wide hips to support a blocky frame. Everything about him was solid and on the big, round-boned face lay a bitter taciturnity. "Anybody could ride an easy chair like Captain Jack."

"Am I braggin' about it?" inquired Kingman.

"Why don't you?" retorted LeTest.

Glance pinned to the foreman, Kingman reached toward his tobacco-sack, saying smoothly: "Wouldn't think of such a thing unless I had your permission." And his later addition was faintly ironic. "I realize you guard the US reputation closely. So do the rest of us working for it. Don't make a damned fool out of yourself, LeTest."

"Might be some argument there," said LeTest rapidly.

Colonel Isom trotted over and leaned down to Kingman.

"It was a ride, Bob. You're in the finals. Now I want you qualifiers up in the Masonic Hall right after dinner to draw for tomorrow's horses. Pujo, Bee Huggins, Harpster, LeTest and Kingman. Don't be foolish tonight and do a lot of drinkin'. The horses don't drink."

Fort Rock's band, hastily assembled on the field, broke into the national anthem. Everybody rose; Colonel Isom turned stiff in the saddle. Kingman pivoted with a military about-face that civilian life could not quite erase and faced the flag slowly going down the halyards at the hands of Jubal Minto. Minto, who had gone up San Juan Hill with Kingman five years back made a ceremony of it. He caught the flag in his arms, never letting it touch the ground; he unsnapped it and folded it and stood still while the music faded out on a long descending note. All at once the crowd broke across the field and the day was done. Kingman turned and walked toward the town, Bee Huggins and Howard Harpster beside him. Neither worked for Running US, but they were ancient friends of Kingman and spoke with friendship's frankness.

"LeTest wouldn't of said that to you," pointed out Harpster, "unless he wanted to develop a fight."

"It's his manner," reflected Kingman. "He's foreman over seventy-five hands and he figures to be a little tougher than they are."

"No," contradicted Harpster. "He's pointed at you. Everybody knows it. You can't go on ignoring him forever. There's a time coming—"

"Listen to me," said Kingman, and stopped in the middle of the walk. The crowd shouldered all three gently to the dusty street. Riders loped past. A restaurant triangle clanged like a fire alarm and the colored squares of Sullivan's Western Star of a sudden blazed with premature lamplight. Down the street tramped the band, making an infernal noise. Kingman nearly shouted. "If the time comes, it will be because mugs like you shove it at us. Nine out of ten gunfights happen just like that. Some fellow squints at another fellow, and the mob yells for action. LeTest figures he's got to be

49

tough. Pretty soon all these rumors about him and me will get the best of his judgment and he'll feel it a point of pride to go through with the affair. You're a couple of blamed fools."

Howard Harpster studied Kingman with bland wisdom. "He never did like you and he's rubbing it in. If you win over him tomorrow he won't feel no better. The man's about got his mind made up there ain't room for both of you on the same map. What happens then? Come on, Bee."

Kingman went on alone to the other side of the street, headed for the restaurant. Near its door he heard his name called and swung back to see Colonel Isom paused opposite with his girl, Frances. Frances waved a pink parasol gaily at Kingman, who started immediately over, but Isom came out into the dust and stopped him there, looking up to Kingman's swept, ruddy cheeks. It was easy to see he had been just such a ridden-slim man as Kingman in his day, as casually certain of himself; and at fifty he showed what Kingman might become. Age had not softened him materially, had not abraded the integral honesty of his make-up. His eyes were that inevitably faded blue which comes of facing many sunrises and sunsets, but they were shrewd, uncompromisingly clear. "I saw you and LeTest jawin' out there," he said. "You're both US riders—and I will not have a squall between you. Mark that down in your little black book."

Kingman smiled. "Supposin' LeTest doesn't agree?"

"I know—I know. He's a hard nut with a one-track mind. Foremen get to be that way, and he's a good one. If he wasn't I wouldn't of kept him all these years. But you ain't the same type, Bob. You've got a brain, and the penalty for havin' a brain is the usin' of it. I'm telling you something I don't want you to forget. A good man never gets anywhere in the world by lettin' himself down to the level of an ordinary hand. Never play the other fellow's game. Play your own."

"A hell of a thing to ask me."

"If I didn't think a lot of you I wouldn't be askin'. Your easy days are done. The sense of the quarrel between you two fellows is so thick around Fort Rock I could cut it with a knife. All right. You've got a decision to make—just to be another fellow that makes his answers in the smoke, or to be somebody worth knowin'. Any fool can be stampeded into gunplay, but it takes a wise man to figure a better way out. Good luck for tomorrow. I'm going to make you ride till your shirt-tail hangs down."

Kingman nodded, moved on. He acknowledged somebody's cheerful greeting and elbowed into the restaurant. Posted on a stool, he checked the bowl of soup that came sliding across the counter to him. He dropped in a handful of oyster crackers, ferried them around with the tip of his spoon, bathed them impartially, absent-mindedly. Somehow irritable, he was thinking that there were points of pride other than Victor LeTest's to be considered here. This affair was like fire in punky wood, eating its secretive way to the surface and there bursting to blaze. He didn't want to fight LeTest, but there was a time when the soft word ceased to be the right word.

2

Rockets were arching brilliantly across the heavens and the holiday crowd made fitful weaving shadows against all the mellow store lights when Bob Kingman walked into the Masonic Hall's stairway and climbed to the upper room. In here was nothing but a confused rumble of voices and a dense fog of tobacco smoke suspended from the ceiling like Spanish moss. All the qualifiers were waiting for him. A roaring dice game operated in one corner, bronzed riders kneeling prayerfully in a circle. There was quite a crowd. Henry Isom came in, holding his hat inverted.

"Every man draws his own horse. You're nearest, Pujo."

Pujo drew and looked. "I get Tonto."

"And Tonto gets you," mused Harpster, stepping up. He drew Roosevelt and shrugged his shoulders. Bee Huggins got Cannonball. Victor LeTest took General Miles. Last to draw, Kingman knew what he had before opening the pellet. It would be Jump-up Joe; it was.

Harpster said: "Huggins and me is out right now. Can't make no show on a couple of hobby horses. We'll hold the stretcher for you, Bob. You picked a lulu."

Pujo nodded his small, dark head at Isom. "Thank you, Colonel," he said courteously. "It was a fair deal—and I got a good bucker."

"You'll stick two jumps," grunted LeTest, unreservedly contemptuous.

Pujo's eyes had a shaded, Latin luminosity to them. They glowed on LeTest. "You," he stated curtly, "are not talking to a US hand. Maybe you can ride horses, but you can't ride me. Cut it out."

A short, strained silence gripped the group. LeTest's broad jaw firmed up as it always did against opposition and he made a motion with his hands. Isom stopped that swiftly. "The remark was uncalled for, LeTest. You boys better get some sleep. The horses don't shoot craps, either."

LeTest wheeled back to the game without further comment and after a moment Pujo followed. Isom said, "Don't do too much dancing tonight, Bob," and went down the stairs, leaving Kingman and Huggins and Harpster to themselves.

"That last crack of Pujo's," said Harpster evenly, "could be construed as a personal reflection on you, Mister Kingman."

"What did I tell you about fool talk?"

Harpster turned impatient. "It's all right to be charitable, my son. But charity begins at home. I'm doggoned if I like to move around the crowd and hear things said about you."

"Things are being said?"

"Things are bein' said."

"So the Romans want a holiday," muttered Kingman.

"If that's the way of the world, can you help it? Never let any man use your reputation to run up his own for bein' tough."

"Why should anybody care?"

Harpster looked to Huggins expressively, then back to Kingman. "It's expected the sun should rise and should set. It's likewise expected you should turn off from nothin' that wears britches."

"Oh, hush."

The dice game fell to pieces in a bitter, explosive quarrel. LeTest reared off his knees and cursed little Pujo, who came straight to his feet and fell against the US foreman with both fists striking out. LeTest shook his head and cursed again. He hit Pujo one square blow, knocked the smaller man against a table. The table capsized and Pujo sank into the wreckage, saying nothing. His breathing cut sharp, slicing echoes into the descended quiet, and he struggled up. LeTest threw himself forward, formidably massive, and punished Pujo with unrelenting right and left smashes to the face. Pujo hit back, frame yielding each time he was struck. He wasn't afraid and he wouldn't give, and for several moments the impact of their fists made a ragged tattoo throughout the room. Then LeTest roared like a bull, broke down Pujo's flimsy barrier, got him beneath the armpits and tossed him ten feet across to a wall. Pujo shook his head wearily and dropped on all fours.

"Get out of here!" shouted LeTest, full of rage. "You beef-stealin' runt—don't come around mixin' with honest people! You got a nerve bein' in Fort Rock at all! Get to hell out of town and back to your brush before US ties you to a tree!"

"You goddam bull," said Pujo, coldly. "You'll never lay your hands on me again!"

"Won't I?" shouted LeTest and moved forward. His solid chin cramped full lips into a downcircling bulldog line; all his face was a dark, rankling mask. "Won't I? Why, I'll throw you down the stairs—"

"Stop that," broke in Kingman. "Settle in your tracks, LeTest."

LeTest stopped in surprise, stared slantwise through the smoke at Kingman. "Who asked you to butt in?"

"When you speak for US you take in too much territory," said Kingman deliberately. "Beat it, Pujo."

Pujo steadied himself against the wall, wiping blood off his cheeks. But he was collected and very calm. "LeTest, you laid your hands on a man one time too many. Maybe you can bullyrag the rest of this country, and maybe you can treat the US riders like a bunch of dogs—"

Kingman broke in gently: "There's some doubt about that, Pujo."

"I don't notice you doubtin' it!"

"Go on—beat it," urged Kingman.

Pujo placed a darkly composed stare on LeTest and departed without hurry. LeTest never bothered to look at him, all this while watching Kingman with a colder concentration. The habitual overbearing contempt roughened his words. "A nice grandstand play, Kingman."

"When you fight you like 'em small, don't you?" said Kingman indolently.

LeTest's cheeks went hard. "I don't draw the line."

"Don't hypnotize yourself with big ideas, LeTest. Your head only holds one fancy at a time."

"You want to correct that fault?" bit off LeTest.

"What your grudge against me is, I don't know. But you've aired it considerable of late. I'm hearing too many things second-hand."

"Here's something first-hand," ground out LeTest. "You never do anything till you get an audience. I don't rate your capacities in any direction worth a damn."

"Fine," applauded Kingman, ironically, "Where do we go from there?"

"It's your corn."

Kingman stared through the smoke, conscious of the drawn-off spectators, of the heavy-weighted interest. The silence in here lay as thick as the smoke. He reached for his tobacco, pushing back the quick and inflammatory words with a self-discipline that was each moment harder to maintain. He was thinking of Colonel Isom's talk which made a barrier aginst his own deep inclinations and he was thinking: "The fool's pride has pushed him into this. How much longer have I got to make allowances?" But his answer was smooth.

"I'll let you make the next move, if you're bound on moving."

LeTest's big lips curled and his attitude was flamboyantly derogatory as he wheeled back to the interrupted game. Kingman only shrugged his shoulders and went down the stairs. On the street Huggins and Harpster reached him.

"The gentle dove of peace," said Harpster, "must be a bad bird."

"He made a mistake usin' his hands on Pujo," said Kingman. "Didn't you see Pujo's eyes?"

"Pujo's a rat."

"Rats bite." He saw both of these old friends caught between loyalty and dissatisfaction. They were moody, depressed; and Harpster was trying to say something. But he checked it. "Never mind. Some hands of poker are harder to play than others."

The aimless ranks of the crowd absorbed and separated them. Kingman lighted his cold cigarette, drew in one breath of smoke, threw it away. The pleasure of the night was gone and that customary ease which comes of a hard day well met refused to abide with him. He was wise enough to realize the symptoms of a troubled conscience. A man had to live with himself, had to keep his own private fences mended; and tonight he had evaded LeTest's plainly issued challenge. "What," he demanded of himself, "has a good brain to do with it? He knocked back my ears and I played I liked it. Hell, this can't go on."

The fiddles and guitars were making melody in the hall above John Loder's store. There was a cluster of men at the stair entry and he passed through with a brief acknowledgment of the friendly approval given him. Somebody said, "Careful of that Jump-up nag, Bob. He ain't got no manners I'm able to discern." When he reached the hall the music had paused and he sighted Frances Isom in a far corner, surrounded by stags. But he reached her as the music started up again, said cheerfully, "Thanks, boys," and wheeled her away. Frances Isom's tall body ended in a glowing copper casque of hair that reached to the level of his chin. She tipped her head to him, quiet amusement in her gray eyes. She had the Isom bearing, the Isom slow certainty written all over the fine, even featuring of her face. It was like her to caution him.

"You shouldn't be dancing. There's tomorrow."

"After tomorrow," said Kingman, "I'm through riding. All this drudgery is just to furnish the home-folks a two-day wallop. The fun's gone out of the game, Frances."

The girl's eyes fell to shining—her smile was that deep and that understanding. "Not you, Bob. As long as there is any strength left in you, you'll be in the middle of things. You were never born to be a spectator."

"You've got me pegged?"

"I had you pegged long ago—long before you knew there was such a girl as me watching you across the corral here. But I wish LeTest had drawn Jump-up Joe instead of you."

"I'd rather lose on a tough horse than win on a bum one."

She said, "We don't want to dance," and led him out of the revolving circle to a quiet corner of the floor. She was suddenly sober, her supple hands folded; and she watched him with a clever, more worried interest. "I heard what happened in the Masonic Hall. I liked your judgment. You did right. Don't let the crowd rush you into something, Bob."

"I wish I knew what ailed the man," muttered Kingman.

"Don't you know? He hates you because of your popularity. Whatever you do interests people. You've got the gift of making fine friends. Every door in Absalom Valley is open to you. Tomorrow all the people in the stands will be pulling for you to win. You're—you're a kind of a hero to this country, Bob."

"Oh, hush."

"That's why he hates you. He's very proud, very powerful. And very lonely, I think. He has no friends. Wherever he goes, your name is ahead of him. Dad likes LeTest because he is a fine foreman. I don't. I think LeTest is a bully

56

who needs one beating to make him human. But the man that does try to beat him takes the chance of being killed. He's a vicious fighter."

"The Romans want a holiday—and your dad wants a mental marvel," grumbled Kingman. "This can't go on much longer."

"Never mind the others," said Frances swiftly. "Do your own figuring. What Bob Kingman does is right, because Bob Kingman does it."

"That goes with you?"

"That goes with me. It always has and always will."

"I bow," said Kingman, grinning.

"And depart. You get a drink and go to bed."

There was no doubt between the two. Her smiling eyes touched him with a private understanding and fell away. Kingman eased down the stairs and passed into the noisy street with a moment's release of care. But it came back again when he entered the packed barroom of Sullivan's Western Star and saw a sign freshly written on the long mirror in heavy soaped letter: "Odds even, Kingman to win over LeTest. A thousand dollars offered."

Kingman beckoned Sullivan. "What in hell have you got that posted for?"

Sullivan's ruby cheeks were amiable, moistly perspiring. He had to lift his voice through the racket. "I can't get it covered. That's what Absalom thinks of you, my lad."

"You're causing trouble."

Sullivan bent over the mahogany. "If it comes, it comes. The situation's beyond you, boy. I know LeTest too well. He's a Texan. If he makes up his mind it stays made. There can't be two number one hands in the Absalom. He knows it. We know it. You ought to."

Kingman turned away abruptly, impatiently. But his path was barred by Tom Vey, who came wheeling his invalid's chair across the floor. Tom Vey's heavy frame was badly shrunken and his hair gray-streaked; his eyes, though, were as canny as they had been in the days of his own riding supremacy.

"Good luck for tomorrow," he told Kingman.

Kingman looked down, knowing Tom Vey would understand. Tom Vey had gone through this a hundred times. "It's my last rodeo, Tom. The fun's gone out of it."

"It always goes," said Vey. "But it comes back when the shoutin's done. As long as you've got sound limbs and good kidneys you'll be waitin' the year through for the battle."

"Like to be out there, Tom?"

Vey's face was dry, expressionless. "I busted my share. One of 'em busted me. No regrets. Part of the game to take what you get, Bob. Good luck for tomorrow."

"Thanks," said Kingman and went back to the street. Turning the corner of the Fort Rock hotel, some odd sight through the boiling crowd arrested his attention. But he didn't immediately look—not until he had gone up the hotel porch and reached the deeper darkness. Then he glanced across the street to a black angle between buildings opposite the Western Star. Pujo stood half concealed in that aperture, watching the saloon's doors.

"LeTest made a mistake hitting that little man," thought Kingman. Alertness pulled his tired muscles together and his thoughts ran along a ready channel of suspicion. A whole succession of streaming rocket light flooded the town with an instant's pale, unnatural radiance and then left the shadows deeper than before. Pujo threw his cigarette into the dust with a nervous motion and turned away. The gesture seemed final; Kingman went into the hotel and walked up to his room. In bed, the problem was very clear to him. He had no sufficient anger to fight LeTest; yet the compulsion of range tradition pushed him inevitably into it. Refusing, he would be ruined. He knew that. A lifetime's reputation for courage could not stand against one moment's show of seeming weakness. Was Isom suggesting that as a greater act? The town band pumped brassy gusts of noise through his window half the night.

3

Pujo was too light to weather the explosive bucking of Tonto. He dusted his breeches on the second jump. Bee Huggins showed daylight and was ruled out, and all the remote spectators in the stands heard his plaintive cursing as he limped back to the mourners' bench. Roosevelt gave Harpster a runaway ride, refusing to make a fight of it. Victor LeTest shot out of the chute with all the earmarks of a fine exhibition under his belt; and then General Miles unexpectedly dumped him. A long "ah" of surprise ran through the crowd. Howard Harpster's Apache yell went skirling into the sultry afternoon air. "Go to it, Bob!"

Kingman balanced himself tentatively on the chute's side and waited for Jump-up Joe to quit fighting the empty saddle. Jump-up Joe was like that—a horse who went mad at the touch of discipline. Nobody liked him; he was a malcontent even in the corral, a fomenter of vicious tooth-and-hoof battles. Kingman lowered himself and swiftly drew back. Jump-up Joe squealed and crashed against the boards. The stands went still and the guardian of the chute gate spoke a warning.

"He'll fiddle like that all afternoon. Drop on him sudden and take your chances. I'll open the gate when I see you grab the hackamore. Be careful—if he thinks of it he'll roll you."

"Now," grunted Kingman and dropped into the saddle. His feet found the stirrups, he seized the hackamore rope. Jump-up Joe, given vent to a display of rage that was almost human, reared up and got his front quarters over the gate before it was quite open. The hand there slashed him across the muzzle with a lariat's end and ducked out of the way. Jump-up Joe came down on the gate and left it so much wreckage behind him. Out across the field he went in a waltzing violence, rising and striking with his forefeet. He squalled again, threw his body half around, whipping Kingman far aside. Kingman scratched him. Kingman cursed him. Jump-up Joe leaped into the sky, all his muscles shuddering; he dropped, and as he dropped he wrenched his long barrel deliberately. It was to Kingman like being on the tip of a curling whip. The bones of his neck cracked and hot fire burned in his stomach. He missed something—he missed the roar of the crowd. Nothing but dead silence announced his ride and into this silence the grunting and the furious snorting of Jump-up Joe made wicked echoes. The horse went to his knees, throwing Kingman's chin against the horn of the saddle; the horse reared and fell into a series of angling, swaying, four-footed plunges. The gun broke with a barking report, the pick-up man drove into Jump-up Joe, and Kingman departed via the rump of the left pick-up man's horse. He stood where he landed, reflexes still churning his brain. Then the fog cleared and the brightness of the day's last sunlight hit his eyes. All the Absalom people were yelling at him. Howard Harpster ran across the field and draped a heavy arm around his shoulders.

"You scrappin' son-of-a-gun!"

The three judges sat together in front of the stands. Colonel Isom called his name and he walked that way, stepping hard against the dirt. Isom held the trophy in his fist and he bent from the saddle and offered it to Kingman with suppressed pride.

"Two years straight for you, Bob. Hang it on your mantel."

"That's one argument settled," said Kingman.

Isom said: "As for the other, play your game, not the other man's."

"His game might be mine."

"Never let Absalom see you do an ordinary thing."

The band broke into the national anthem and everybody rose. The flag fluttered down. This was the end of it for another year. Gone loose and weary, Kingman told himself there could never be another year. He should be pleased, he should be feeling that relaxing glow of physical ease. But he wasn't feeling it. He stood there, with his mind locked in the insoluble problem LeTest presented. The fine edge of recklessness no longer cut his difficulties for him, there was no swift answer as there once had been. The trouble was—and

60

the realization hit him hard—he saw two sides to this affair; and when a man came to that stage he was old and the fun was out of the game.

The music crashed out into the silence and ceased. Jubal Minto strode by with the folded flag in his arms. Steve Mountjoy raced away from a lighted fuse in the center of the field and a moment later the crashing explosion of powder confined between anvils went tearing into the suddenly sunless air. It was all over. Kingman wheeled toward Fort Rock's street; Howard Harpster fell into step.

"Tonight," said Kingman, "we'll christen this cup."

"Well, don't cry about it."

"The prospects don't sound as joyous as of yore, Howard," said Kingman irritably, and went off alone. It was beyond six. He ate, the trophy tucked inconspicuously on his lap; later he went to the hotel room. For a little while he lay flat on the bed, hearing the Fourth of July fireworks sputter and snap below him. The band was tirelessly, terribly in operation again. "So, because he is a fool full of pride," muttered Kingman, "and I'm a fool with another kind of pride, we fall to a killing. Two years ago it wouldn't of mattered. But now it seems all wrong."

It was dusk when he walked down to the street. The sprinkling cart had been by and the acrid odor of dampened dust was strong in the air. Store lights made brilliant patches through the windows; restless eddies of people surged against each other, dissolved, reformed. There was the sound of high revelry in Sullivan's Western Star. When Kingman walked in the full force of it turned on him, hit him with a warm, healthy friendliness. For that one moment a sense of comfort dissolved the hard core of resenting uncertainty in him. He smiled at all those riding partners, laid the cup on the bar.

"As long as there's any man standing on his feet, Sullivan," he drawled, "keep that thing full."

A long yell engulfed him. But Howard Harpster came forward and his grave resistance to the holiday mood brought

61

a silence. Harpster's words were almost metallic.

"I wouldn't do any drinkin' Bob. LeTest has been extending his remarks."

"You're a fool, Howard."

Harpster said doggedly: "That's all right. Call me anything you want. But I'd rather see you dead than make the wrong answer. You're Kingman, see? Don't forget that. Some things you've got to do."

Kingman looked into his partner's hard, anxious eyes and some odd chemical change happened in him, dissolved the puzzle and left him recklessly satisfied. He said to himself, "I can't change from what I used to be," and then he answered Harpster. "I shall have to take care of whatever comes my way."

The straining look on Harpster's face broke. "That's it," he half cried. "I—"

He got no farther. The saloon doors shrilled and a body passed rapidly in, bearing heavily on the floor. Kingman turned casually and saw LeTest come to a stiff, stubborn stand. LeTest had heard and Kingman knew then that his slow phrase had crystallized the foreman's anger beyond change. LeTest's bitter, jealous eyes hit Kingman.

"All the outfit goes back to the ranch tonight. Get your horses and go."

It was nothing but an expedient to climax the quarrel. Any other would have done. This was showdown, and there was nothing left now but the old, timeless ceremony of acceptance. Kingman said:

"I'm staying here."

"You've got ten minutes," rapped out LeTest. "If I find you in town after that you know what to expect." He turned then and walked rapidly from the room.

Kingman pushed the trophy cup, farther across the bar. "Keep it full," he repeated, and followed LeTest to the street. Paused there, he found no sight of the US foreman, but his name was briskly called and he turned to see Tom Vey wheeling himself from the saloon. Vey's prematurely old face seemed very tired.

"I'd hate to see you go through with this."

"What would you do?" challenged Kingman.

"If I had your body I'd do just what you're going to do," admitted Vey. "But I'm not rough and tough any more and it looks different to me. You're both good men, Bob. A bullet settles nothing and leaves one of you dead."

"LeTest is of age."

"LeTest is his own worst enemy. He's proud and he won't give."

"So I ought to do the givin'?"

"He'd go through hell to be a popular man, which is why he hates you. He'd cut off both arms to help a friend."

"What friends?"

"I'm his friend," murmured Vey. "The only one he's got, I guess. Once upon a time I was his sort of a fellow."

"The thing is settled, Tom."

Vey's tone was inexpressibly regretful. "Men make a lot of unnecessary trouble for each other."

Kingman crossed the street and went to his room. He strapped on his gun-belt, lifted the weapon from its seat, dropped it lightly back. He made one moody turn of the room, thinking of the sadness of Vey's answer, thinking of this futile ending just ahead. And then he closed his mind to thinking and walked out. Frances Isom was on the shadowed porch, waiting for him. She came forward, she touched him gently with one hand.

"You're sure this is what you want to do, Bob?"

All the contradictions angered him. He was sharp, almost severe. "Tell your dad there's other things besides a good mind."

"That was his way of telling you he didn't want to lose you, Bob. This is my way—"

She lifted, kissed him. "But I said last night your way was my way." She was crying. Crying bitterly. He started to speak, and found the porch empty. Frances ran down the steps and into the crowd. Searching for her with his eyes, he suddenly saw Pujo in the far shadows, in that black niche he had been in the evening before. Covertly drawn back, the little man was again turned toward the Western Star.

Kingman felt a sense of needed hurry, of overhanging disaster. It came upon him without explanation and carried him off the steps into the street. He crossed, entered a stable and passed to its rear; he cut through another alley and placed himself to command Pujo from a different angle. "LeTest," he thought, "made a mistake hitting that fellow."

Some shift of Pujo's body warned him and he looked around to discover LeTest striding along the dust, bound for the Western Star. The word was published, that much was plain from the manner in which the edges of the crowd recoiled. There was less noise in the saloon; men hurried out and swiftly edged aside. LeTest came slowly on and paused at the doors, all his motions controlled by that weighted care of one balanced on the fine edge of action. Kingman watched him with a blacker and blacker temper; and then he returned his hard glance to Pujo. The little man had crawled from the recess. He lifted his gun with a strange, gliding sureness—setting its sights against LeTest who stood unaware sixty feet away. Kingman thought savagely, "He's not intendin' to give LeTest a chance," and afterward his racing hand dropped and rose and fired. The sound made a rending, crashing blast between the building walls. A woman screamed. Pujo never let a word out of him, but he staggered into a lane of light, quick agony slashing deep lines into his thin face. One arm hung broken and the fingertips turned to a flowing crimson. Victor LeTest's voice rode the night with a fierce, bitter anger.

"I'll finish this—"

"Shut up!" called Kingman. "You had it coming. Pujo, get out of town!"

Men streamed from the Western Star. Howard Harpster's giant frame laid a great patch against the saloon's glow and the dying fragments of talk struck unnaturally clear into the pervading suspense. LeTest and Kingman and Pujo formed a motionless triangle, but Pujo was a limp, beaten man with a bleak fear on his cheeks and at that moment Kingman felt a pity—a remote pity. His own body squared itself against the US foreman.

"Your ten minutes are up, LeTest. If you are going to draw, do it now."

LeTest's face was dim. The hulking frame shifted. "You did me a favor," he said in a wondering voice.

"Never mind that."

"You had no reason to step in here, Kingman."

Kingman said brusquely: "I don't deal in murder. The ten minutes are up."

But LeTest was rooted and perplexed; and Kingman got a faint view of that broadly formidable face oddly cast. LeTest's hanging arms drew up, a motion of resignation. "No—you've done me a favor."

"I don't claim it," said Kingman sharply.

"I never go back on my obligations," grumbled LeTest.

For a moment nothing was said; the ranked people were rigidly absorbed in this scene turned strange beyond reason. Kingman's hat brim jerked sharply upward and one hand described a final gesture.

"This thing has got to end here. I see no point in a gunfight, LeTest. But it is either that or no more talk of a quarrel between us."

"Kingman," exploded LeTest, "you're a damned sight better man than I figured!"

Kingman shifted, moved forward. "We'll drink on that, LeTest!"

"I'm your friend," said the US foreman.

Sudden motion swept the crowd off Fort Rock's walks. Howard Harpster emitted an Apache yell and came up to strike LeTest soundly on the back. Colonel Isom walked out of the crowd and he said proudly: "Kingman, you never do the ordinary thing." Then he turned to the crowd, deeply pleased. "The men of my outfit are loyal. The drinks are on me tonight!"

Kingman looked across the street to Frances standing straightly against the hotel wall, saw the shining approval of her eyes. He extended his hand to LeTest, a fine sense of

65

ease and recklessness running beneficently through him. "Next year," he drawled, "we'll give those horses a better ride."

IMPORTANT QUESTION

Hugh Carroll came down the street on his long-legged sorrel, gave Silver Bob a young man's cheerful grin and passed out of town by the Gila Butte road; at Toweep Wash he turned left.

There were times in the sheriff's life when a good deal of patient waiting came to a sudden point, as now. Noting Hugh Carroll's direction, Silver Bob got his horse from the stable, circled southward through the broken land and thereafter settled down to a hot afternoon's ride across the silver and gray and bronze flash of the desert floor.

Little things always added up if a man was patient enough to wait, and the sheriff was a patient man, made gray and wise and cool by the years. Hugh Carroll was a red-headed youngster who had grown up in this country. He was a little bit wild and headstrong and, like many another kid, time got heavy on his hands and lately he had been riding westward over the desert. By this traveling and by other little indications, the sheriff knew Carroll was meeting Sam Brett somewhere yonder. And Sam Brett was a tough one the sheriff wanted.

The sheriff knew this land as he knew the palm of his hand. Men could camp only where water was; and the kid's direction indicated a meeting place east and south of the Willows. Weighing certain imponderables in his head, Silver Bob made his guess and at dusk of a long, yellow-hot afternoon he reached Dead Man's Camp and threw off his saddle beside a small spring in the rock outcrop. He had never met Sam Brett, who was recently from New Mexico, but he had the outlaw's description.

Short, bare hills rose near him and a mesquite thicket skirted the water hole. The fire made a pale, steady cone in a night that closed down black and solid. Crouched before the flame, Silver Bob used an old can to boil up some coffee, and presently heard the scuff of a pair of horses coming off the hills. The riders stopped somewhere in the mesquite and he knew they were watching him, but of this he gave no sign. Presently, looking up from his coffee, he found the pair across the fire. One of them was thin and sick—with wickedness ground into his face. The other was over six feet and wore a sheepherder's black hat. This, the sheriff knew at once, was Sam Brett.

Silver Bob said: "Howdy," in his soft, undisturbed voice and gestured at the coffeepot. He sat by the flame, tapering up a cigarette, and his eyes looked into the heart of the fire and showed the newcomers no interest. But he was thinking that Sam Brett was a hard case and that Sam Brett's partner made the situation a little complicated. The dust and weariness of a long ride was on both of them as they settled opposite. Sam Brett's fist, reaching for the coffeepot, showed its scarred, solid knuckles. He drank his coffee straight from the pot, with a little of the coffee spilling down the corners of his lips.

There was another horse coming through the mesquite, and then the rider entered the bright cell of light and said, "Hello, Sam," and afterward Silver Bob turned on his heel and watched young Hugh Carroll's face grow smooth and grave—covering shock.

Sam Brett said, to Carroll: "Hello." Nothing more. But the sheriff, drowsing before the fire, read a question and a warning in that one word. As though Sam Brett, a stranger in the country, was asking information of Carroll, who knew the land and everybody in it. Young Carroll, crouched at the edge of the flame, drew a mesquite branch along the earth, making idle figures there; and at once Silver Bob understood that the kid, at this stage of the game, wouldn't give him away. He had known Carroll from childhood, and this was what stopped Hugh Carroll's tongue—a lingering loyalty to a man who was his friend. It was the way the game was played.

There was a shadow sweeping up from the desert, and the swift run of another rider who hailed the fire with a single, deep call before approaching it. Afterward this man dropped from his pony and came into the light and crouched over the pool and drank with greedy, gusty sweeps of breath. He said, "Hot day," and moved around and sat on the vacant side of the fire. Crouched down, he searched the group with a single dark survey—the sheriff, the kid and the two outlaws. No recognition stirred him, though as owner of all the surrounding range this Ben Dade knew the sheriff and Hugh Carroll, and could make his plain guesses at the two strangers.

The sheriff's long, half-frail fingers lay across his bent knees. The smoke of the cigarette drifted before his eyes and a dreaming peace composed his expression. Brett's eyes were round and black and bright, across the fire. They held Silver Bob in a steady, speculative scrutiny. This man, Silver Bob thought, was a tough and quick one, who had been bad a long time and knew all the tricks.

All things worked out, one way or another. There were certain rules a man could go by. The water hole had drawn them here, and in due time, if nothing was said, they would rise and go their separate ways, silently and without trouble. And, according to the rules of the game, neither Hugh Carroll nor Ben Dade would ever speak of it afterward to Silver Bob.

But the sheriff wanted Sam Brett and so he closed this honorable avenue of retreat behind him. Crouched and silent and gentle-faced he had his thoughts, all close and

69

quick. It wasn't Brett that troubled him or made him give this situation so deep and prolonged an attention. It was Brett's partner that made it difficult. Silently there on the ground, he placed each man in proper relation. Brett would draw at the first word, for Brett was a tough one; and the partner would draw. Ben Dade would not come into this. Ben was an honest man, but Ben had his own ethics; and this was not Ben's quarrel.

It depended, then, on the kid. If the kid was still sound he would block Brett's partner; if he had turned bad he wouldn't move—and it would be the bullet of Brett's partner that would knock him, Silver Bob, down to the dust.

And suddenly in this silence, all of them knew that. There was a smell here that Brett and his partner had caught; Brett's black round eyes drilled across the top of the flame like the dismal apertures of a shotgun, centered on Silver Bob. Brett's partner stirred gently on his heels and his open mouth began to close, slowly. Ben Dade's face was taciturnly motionless behind his cigarette smoke; and Hugh Carroll's expression showed faint strain. They were four men sharing this knowledge, each one gravely waiting through the slow moments.

Silver Bob finished his cigarette, his fingers supporting it, and tossed it into the dying coals.

"All right, Brett."

He drew as he spoke, knowing his man; and his bullet caught Brett's shoulder as the latter's arm swept up with a gun. Brett wheeled backward, knocked off balance, and Hugh Carroll's body shot across the light and struck Brett's partner down. Ben Dade sighed and threw his cigarette into the flames, and the smoke of Silver Bob's gun was a rank taint around all of them. That was all there was. Brett pulled himself back to his heels, one arm clapped to his struck shoulder. He stared at the sheriff in the resigned, unangered way of a man who had gambled too many years to cry at the wrong turn. In his voice, when he spoke, was the admiration

70

of one expert for another; it was a kind of professional tribute:

"Your judgment, friend, is pretty sharp. I had it figured the other way."

HANG UP MY GUN

All afternoon Jastrow Brant, the pressure of whose big body against a lame hip had long since tamed him to a chair, sat on the porch of his High Pass tavern and watched the inevitable signals of another range war rise from the bald and tawny domes around him. Situated on the exact summit of the range, the world was for him an unrolling scene; below to the west the immense dun flatness of the Yellow Horn country—a feuding domain of cattle kings— marched league upon league into the horizon, overcast by a sultry heat haze that was itself like a portent of trouble. The sun was a shapeless glow in the sky; eastward on the other side of the range the slashed and contorted badlands had a sulphur-bronze-platinum coloring, all the false beauties of its chemicals beckoning the inexperienced traveler into the labyrinthian trap.

Still, it was out of the western range and into the badlands that hurrying riders were this afternoon urging their jaded horses. First had come a mere youth, so agitated that he galloped past the watering trough unmindful. Since it was the only water for sixty miles east, Brant called a warning and had no reply excepting a startled backward glance. "Fool kid on a Diamond-and-a-half pony, and he'll lose the pony pretty soon," murmured Brant, considering him to be a fugitive from some solitary scrape, but later three other horsemen came up from the Yellow Horn to revise his opinion. These men also straddled Diamond-and-a-half ponies, and though they were more experienced and not too rushed to halt for water, Brant observed the uneasiness in them.

They said nothing and were soon gone. "Bad feelin's busted out again," he murmured. "Looks like Diamond-and-a-half is gettin' licked." Within the hour a fellow astride a sweat-caked Cloverleaf roan drifted by, one arm hanging useless. Scarce had he disappeared down the throat of the pass when a sizable group, composed of Y Cross men, all looking hostile, rounded a high dome to the southward and advanced on the tavern. They were not hunted, his judging eye told him, but hunters; and the leader was known to him as Toomey, the Y Cross foreman.

"Seen anything, Brant?"

"No," said Brant. "I never see anything. You know that, Toomey."

"Hell's broke loose again," offered Toomey with a visible deference, "and we're payin' off." There was a stifled consultation among them and when the watering was done they moved away, not along the trail but into the higher buttes north of the tavern. "You ain't seen us at all, Brant," called back the foreman.

Brant made a logical pattern of the gleaned facts. "Diamond-and-a-half and Cloverleaf buckin' the Y Cross, which is usual. And Y Cross holdin' its own, also usual. But it looks bad. Can't change the habits of twenty years makin'. These outfits are plumb poison to each other and they love to scrap. Evident the battle's been on two-three days. The boys are rid tired, full of dust and sweated out."

Afterward, Y Cross having been gone an hour, a wary fugitive shot from a crease of the hills, dashed for water and was away. A great golden shaft of the sun finally broke through the haze and exploded against the range in a thousand glinting fragments. And at this interval, framed in the blazing shield of light, tall and supple and indolent in the saddle, the smiling man came along.

He came not from the Yellow Horn country but east out of the badlands, whereupon Brant knew he had traveled far during the day. The horse was a high black, streaked with alkali, and all the gear was worn and plain. Rounding to the trough, the smiling man let the horse nose into the water, himself dismounting and pushing back his hat to reveal corn-colored hair that instantly added a candid cast to features molded against a deeply tanned skin. Actually he wasn't smiling, but the level serenity of his glance and the puckered sun-wrinkles around each eye seemed to create an air of constitutional cheer. His movement was lazy, deliberate. He crouched and drank beside the horse. He rose with a sighing relish and planted his feet apart in puncher's style. He weighed his surroundings with a bland, half-lidded glance; then, these preliminaries complete, he spoke a brief and drawling phrase that swept aside the ordinary explanations as if indicating them to be a waste of energy. "Sit tight. I'll stable the horse myself." And he led it around to the barn. The brand mark was strange to Brant, being a 44 Slash and probably southern on account of its size. He was searching the capacious archives of his memory when the stranger returned and settled on the steps, reaching for tobacco.

"This day," he said, yellow head bent over the chore of rolling a smoke, "sure has been a weariness to the spirit and flesh."

"So," agreed Brant. As in horse, so in man; breeding showed. This stranger was no wandering scrub. He had loosely coupled members and a torso that ran admirably from slim flanks to a broad, flat chest. The fingers displayed deftness in rolling the cigarette; there was a single gun, carried low enough to indicate wisdom in the draw. The eyes of the man, casually turning on Brant, were infinitely more capable of hardness than first inspection had revealed. About him was an ease, a touch of reckless assurance.

"Down there," he added, "even the rattlers are huntin' shade." After a pause he added, "and some men," chuckling a little to himself. Cigarette smoke curled over his face; he relaxed limply on the steps. Shadows came into the world and suddenly the blue banners of dusk drifted around. A gust of fresher air touched them as promise of the usual crisp, high-altitude night. Inside the tavern was a light rhythm of steps, lamp glow gushed through the door and a woman's voice called: "Supper."

The stranger's indolence vanished. He rose, flipped away the cigarette and turned, catching sight of a bright dress moving within the tavern. "Better scrub some," said he and moved toward the trough, untying his neckpiece. Brant went inside. The stranger presently followed, to find man and girl waiting at the table. Standing there, beads of water sparkling on the yellow hair and the selfsame glint of humor in his level eyes, he seemed to feel the necessity of manners before breaking bread with these people. "My name," he announced, "is Lewis Cantrell. From the Poco country."

"I'm Jastrow Brant," said the tavern keeper. "My daughter, Lee Ann. Sit and fall to. Ridin' makes a man hungry."

"Which gives me license to eat well," replied Cantrell, turning to the girl. "I've been ridin' all my life."

"Yeah," agreed Brant. "I know that lean and gaunt feelin' and I'd give most of my possessions to have it again. When I was young the whole universe was too small to turn in. Not now. I been a rockin' chair rider for twenty years."

Surprise ran deeply through him. Lewis Cantrell's pleasant face had turned to Lee Ann, and this slim, dark girl, who invariably met tavern guests with grave reserve, smiled at him. It was like a spark flashing out; something strange and very powerful entered the room to lighten the gloom and the dullness of the place. Youth and youth. Brant felt anew the hurt of being old. He studied the stranger through harder eyes, a kind of defensive cruelty in his heart. "You've gadded some, eh?"

"My feet burn if I stay in one place long," agreed Cantrell. "I take no pride in it. I only say it for a fact."

"Some run because they like it, some because they got to."

Cantrell grinned and the characteristic chuckle made a little melody through the room. "In my case it's mostly from like, but now and then necessity."

Brant looked at his daughter, expecting that she, who hated lawlessness with more than passing reason, would draw back. Instead, she asked a swift, eager question. "You love that life?"

Lewis Cantrell sobered. "I have thought it fine to rove and lay my blanket under the sky. It's good to have weather in your face and a sound horse under you, puttin' miles behind. It's great—until something hits you between the eyes and you see maybe you've only been a fool."

Lee Ann's glance rested levelly on him. "What would make you feel that?"

"A man's self-sufficient just as long as he thinks he is," said Cantrell. "I have figured I could ride forever, one long and full day. But sometimes I see down the trail and it looks cloudy at the end. Lone riders are like lone wolves—they howl out in the hills awhile and then they don't howl any more. Nobody hears or sees them again."

Lee Ann's lips curved up at the corners. "You came smiling. Now you are sad. Our house seems bad medicine for you."

They watched each other for quite a long interval. "Maybe good medicine," said Cantrell.

The chill of night increased in the room. Brant pushed his plate away and rose to drop a match on the kindling in the fireplace. He sank into his accustomed chair, a darker glow rising from beneath his brows. Lee Ann busied herself at the table and Lewis Cantrell stood facing the fire, attention absorbed in the crimson core of flame. Brant, ruthless when on a scent, began to question the man. "Forty-four Slash is new to me."

"Rodd Brothers ranch, western Kansas," said Cantrell absently.

"Only business could bring you through the badlands on a day like this."

"Business, yes."

"But now you tarry," grunted Brant.

"Waitin' out the business," drawled Cantrell and roused himself. "It's maybe a tough country through here?"

"Sometimes."

"I wondered how it was you kept from bein' bothered."

Lee Ann came from the kitchen and sat down. Daughter

76

and father exchanged a quiet glance. "I'm let alone," answered Brant, somewhat abrupt.

Cantrell laced his arms behind and lifted his inspection to a belt with two attached guns hanging over the mantel. The belt was black with usage, the weapons freshly oiled. "Those," said he, following an interested survey, "were used by a man who knew how."

Brant's answer was increasingly curt. "Left in payment of a bad debt."

"Ahuh," agreed Cantrell, so mild as to echo skepticism.

They heard the impact of a galloping horse outside. The rider drew in by the house and instantly Cantrell's hand rose, remaining thus attentive until the unseen traveler pushed on eastward. Thereafter the knit intentness of his forehead gave way, but both Brant and Lee Ann, watching closely, had seen how easily the air of indifference could drop from this man. It prompted Brant to another question.

"Know the Yellow Horn country?"

"Some little," said Cantrell and let it go at that.

The girl rose, went through a far door and presently returned with a pair of slippers; she helped her father remove his boots and get into the slippers. Cantrell looked down, darker of face than he had thus far been, and the girl, meeting his eyes, unexpectedly challenged him. "Does it hit you so hard?"

"My life," said he, almost bitter, "has led me to believe these things, woman and house and warm fire, are for the blessed alone. I have not known them."

"Never for you—never?"

"Time for bed," said Cantrell abruptly and turned away.

Lee Ann brought another lamp from the kitchen and led him up the stairs to a room. At the door he took the lamp and held her eyes for a moment. There was between them the constraint of withheld words and in the long pause a rising fire of emotion that flickered and flamed; then the girl, stronger color on her temples, nodded and turned back. Cantrell closed the door, scowling at the exact neatness of the room, the bed with its folded coverlet, the net curtains stiff beside the window. Extinguishing the lamp, he went to the window and scanned the dark earth. A quarter moon shed a crescent light on the yard and touched briefly the mystery-ridden domes beyond. Watching and listening for a space, he at last laid himself on the bed fully dressed and brought the coverlet over him, not to sleep but to stare at the black square of ceiling. "A woman like that," said he, half aloud, "will never bring slippers to me."

Below in the big room, Jastrow Brant shot a swift question at his daughter. "You like him, Lee Ann?"

"Yes," said she, breath rising. "I do."

Brant frowned at the fire. "Can't blame you. You've had nothin' but the company of an old man since you was a kid. You're starved for company your own age."

"Don't forget, there have been young men here before— and I haven't liked them."

Brant rose, endeavoring to conceal the discontent in him. "Seems like I get sleepy mighty soon these days. Well, he's better than average. That I know. He's maybe eaten a lot of beef not his own, but he ain't a killer type."

"Of course he isn't! That name—"

"But he's up here for a reason," interrupted Brant, and went to his room. Settled down for the night he considered Lewis Cantrell with a restless mind. Lee Ann passed softly down the hall and silence settled. Still awake an hour later, Brant heard a horseman canter into the yard and halt; a short whistle, twice repeated, hailed the house and presently Cantrell came down the stairs. Crawling from his bed, Brant limped to the window, finding the two men close together just beyond the porch, talking in undertones. It lasted only a moment; when the newcomer swung away a stray beam of moonlight slid across his face and revealed it. Lewis Cantrell came inside and walked up the stairs with no attempt at being furtive.

Sudden savagery lived in Jastrow Brant's veins—an emotion he had not felt since active manhood. His peaceful life had been painfully built up and here in the space of a single afternoon it was threatened. "Frawley," he muttered, "the

78

Cloverleaf ridin' boss, comes here to meet Cantrell by appointment. Cantrell's got a hand in that war yonder. He's a gun slinger, nothin' less. And my girl wants him. I saw it in her eyes. Wants him regardless of price. Damn the man, I'll see him dead before I'll let him drag Lee Ann down to an outlaw's level!"

But whatever hard resolves were in him he held his peace next morning until Cantrell, having curried his pony, strolled onto the porch; this was to be a waiting game then. Brant rubbed his leg and broke a spell of thoughtful silence.

"Cantrell. Was a man in Yellow Horn once by that name. He had Y Cross for awhile."

Cantrell turned a javelin-sharp glance on him. "You knew that man?"

Brant was smoking a cigar. He drew on it vigorously and the heavy clouds of smoke obscured his face. After a considerable pause he said. "Somewhat."

"My father," explained Cantrell. "A great and good man who believed all other men were as honest as himself." Terrible cynicism crept into the words. "He abided by the Golden Rule in a country of stalkin' savages. Yonder is the Y Cross tank. My father built it. He settled and developed the Y Cross range. It was his and he put the best of his years in it. I was born there and for seven years it was the only happy world I ever knew or ever will know. The rest of the story is no doubt familiar to you."

"He was killed twenty years ago this October," said Brant.

"By yellow curs who wanted what he had and were afraid of tacklin' him alone. So they organized a war and killed him. The owners today are those men. I was a kid when I left. My mother died soon after. I been driftin' ever since."

"But you're back now," murmured Brant.

"I'm back now," said Cantrell in a manner that was more of a threat than a statement. His slim face, pointed at the dim outlines of the Y Cross water tower, was hard and predatory. "They made a lone wolf out of me."

"The hates of men," said Brant, "make a hell of this earth that could be forever at peace."

Cantrell swung on the tavern keeper. "That sounds like you got it from yourself and not from a book. It's true. But a single rider like me can't feel it very deep, true as it may be."

"Not yet," sighed Brant. "Not yet."

There was a sound at the door. Both men turned to see Lee Ann retreating hurriedly into the big room. Jastrow Brant pushed himself from the chair and limped around the barn. When he came back it was to say briefly, "Got to shake up my liver," and to disappear southward into a disappearing crease of the hills; midafternoon had passed before he returned, sagging with weariness. Cantrell was out of sight. Lee Ann, answering her father's first question, motioned to the barn. "There, with his horse. Where have you been?"

"Answering my own questions," groaned Brant and sank into the rocker. "Judas, what wouldn't I give for a sound body. Lee Ann, I ought to have died when that bullet smashed this hip! I ought to have died!"

"Hush!"

Brant pulled himself together with a vast heave of shoulders. "I'm too old a dog not to know. The country yonder is full of single rider's tracks, all driftin' out of the badlands and collectin' somewhere. An unexpected strike at Y Cross, that's the idea. It explains Frawley of Cloverleaf comin' to meet Cantrell. Those are Cantrell's men. He means to get even with his dad. Another bitter bloody scrap like in the old days."

"He can't do that!" said the girl, clenching her hands.

"You talked with him whilst I was away?"

"Ye-es."

The old man studied her closely and finally shook his head. "I was hopin' for better news. I know you, Lee Ann. You've got my blood and you want what you want, regardless of price."

"Not an outlaw!" said Lee Ann, all her strength in the words. "Never—never!"

Brant said nothing, but in his mind was a doubt. The

80

blood of his family had always been a little wild. Once sworn to allegiance it never wavered. His own crippled body testified to the fact, and the same steadfast blindness would break Lee Ann's heart. Discouraged and irritable, he ate a bite in the kitchen and went to his room for a nap. It was on his mind to go speak to Cantrell plainly but a stronger quality in him overruled the impulse. He hated interferences and he understood Cantrell's kind. Nothing he might say would change the long-crystallized fighting desire that had brought the man back to his birthplace. So, troubled of mind and body, he fell into a restless slumber.

When he woke there was a crisp clashing of voices in the yard. Cantrell was speaking with a metal-edged drawl. "Who I am and where I'm going is my business."

"My business if I make it so," said an equally hard voice. Brant rose so abruptly that an idling heart pounded in protest. When he reached the porch he found Cantrell confronting the Y Cross patrol party. Toomey's hostility diminished on sight of Brant. "Listen, we been keepin' an eye on this road and this man. Jastrow, I want no grief with you but yo're foolish to harbor trouble."

"Never mind Brant," said Cantrell definitely. "I stay here because it is a public place. Don't lay any pressure on me, brother. I've been on ridin' committees myself and I know the old soap."

"Yuh come up from the badlands," accused Toomey.

"What of it?"

"Bear this in mind, mister. Here's a dividin' line. We'll agree yore business is yores, this side of the line. Step over inside Yellow Horn and we'll pick you up."

"Get out of here," growled Brant.

Toomey's manner was half uneasy and half insistent. "No personal affront, Brant, but I got my orders. Come on, boys."

The party swept downgrade into the Yellow Horn, now all smoky with the last of the afternoon's turgid light. Brant watched them until the last trailing horseman vanished beyond a curve. Cantrell walked around the house and in a little while led back his horse. "I put you under suspicion and I'm sorry," said he. "I'll be on my way pretty soon and relieve you of worry."

"South, I reckon," suggested Brant, sinking into the rocker.

Cantrell cast a hard blue glance at him. "I figured from the first you didn't miss much. South it is."

"How do you suppose I've lived the last forty-five years?" muttered Brant, unfavoring. "I've seen 'em come and go. Many that went down there never came back. Some did come back, marked to die. Fools like you, Cantrell! Fools like you!"

"Have I said I wasn't?" retorted Cantrell.

"That's what makes it sad to me. You ain't of the ordinary run of shad. You got a heart and a head. You got the breeding of a stout, sound man. But—I will not keep you, Cantrell. Yonder is your signal!"

Cantrell lifted his head. Off on the southern slopes a rider emerged and sent his horse in widening circles. Cantrell rose, deep feeling rushing over his face and passing on to leave it chilled and bleak. "I'd like to shake hands, Brant."

Brant's big paws remained on the rocker arms. "Get out of here!"

Cantrell climbed to his saddle, slim fingers idling on the reins. "I shouldn't't come here," said he. "It's brought back to me things a lone wolf never ought to think about—things only so much misery to a man dodgin' from pillar to post—"

Lee Ann ran through the door and down the steps. She laid an arm on the horse's mane and looked up at Cantrell. Brant, almost ceasing to breathe, felt dull grief that a daughter of his should so throw herself away by every gesture and expression.

"You're going?" asked Lee Ann, faint and small.

Lewis Cantrell swept off his hat, the last flash of sun rolling up tawny flames on his head. "Going, Lee Ann."

"Nothing that has happened here matters to you?"

He stared down, mouth pressed thin. "I can't answer that."

"Nothing I might say now would change your mind?"

"Better do it this way, though God knows it's bad enough," said Cantrell, and at that moment even Brant felt a touch of compassion for the man. But he was shocked inexpressibly by the sweep of wild anger distorting the girl's white cheeks—an anger that was actually hate.

"Then go!" she cried at Cantrell, and struck the horse with her doubled fist. "Go on, you—you outlaw! But never set your foot in our house again!"

Lewis Cantrell bowed and whirled away, sweeping up the rising terrain; the sun sank and instant tendrils of dusk filtered through the sky. Yonder the messenger waited in plain view but Cantrell saw him only dimly, through a deepening cloud, and when he came abreast the man he never stopped. Plunging into the deeper recesses he turned for a last glance at the tavern. The girl still stood in the yard, a rigid, diminishing figure. Cantrell stiffened to the front. "Better that way," he muttered. "Better one single hurt than dragged out regretted misery all her life. I'm the kind to ruin the happiness of all I touch. But, by God, it's hard to do!"

The messenger spurred forward. "What's the matter, Lew?"

"Nothing!" shouted Cantrell. "Shut your mouth!"

They galloped side by side down the gulch. Dusk deepened, and when half an hour later they came into a depression of the earth, the murmuring impatience of a heavy group of waiting men met them. Without an order, the whole outfit swung up. A figure rode forward and Frawley of Cloverleaf spoke. "Ready to go?"

Cantrell studied the dim torsos around him. Frawley had brought along ten Cloverleaf hands and these he didn't know. But he knew his own crowd. Once they had seemed good enough. Now, in a flash of clarity, he discovered they were the sweepings of the West, collected to destroy and plunder. They could be no better than that, for he himself had picked them.

"Ready to go?" pressed Frawley.

"We'll ride," said Cantrell in a dull voice and moved

ahead. Behind him grew the steady beat of the party, a sickle moon glowed ineffectively, and across the infinite heaven was a crusted glitter of stars. By degrees a semi-permanent group of lights strengthened on the prairie below—the still far-off lamps of Y Cross. Frawley said in a softening rumble, "Swing right here. Tell your bunch not to make so much noise."

Cantrell heard himself say, "Draw up!"

The party passed him and came around in grumbling surprise. Frawley swore. "Now what?"

"Who's down there at the ranch?" asked Cantrell, feeling himself thrust upward on the wings of a cold, unfathomable exultance.

"Part of a crew and one of the owners, Crow Hicks. Don't worry. I've took care of my end of this business."

Cantrell shook his head, seeing odd shapes come out of the black frame of night; there was a fire leaping from a hearth, a woman kneeling in front of it with slippers in her white hands. "As maybe is happenin' in the Y Cross house now," said he. "Why didn't I think of it before?"

"What?" inquired Frawley, more and more impatient.

"Frawley," said Cantrell, still and cold, "I'm through."

"Listen, you," breathed Frawley, coming nearer, "after three months of plannin' you ain't goin' to develop no weak heart. Come on."

"We're drawin' out," ordered Cantrell.

"Damn you, don't crawl!" cried the Cloverleaf boss.

Cantrell cleared the surrounding men and placed himself downslope against them. Frawley cursed and the whole ragged outline of the party shifted nearer. Cantrell was swayed by a strangely savage emotion that seemed to clear his head of every atom of bitterness and uncertainty. He was right, his thoughts ran in a true channel at last. The machine he had so painstakingly built to accomplish destruction was now on the verge of riding him down and he didn't care; in the dark his lips curled into a kind of smile.

"Push that fool aside!" yelled Frawley.

"Don't trust him behind us," countered another voice. "Take him along."

"I organized you hammerheads," droned Cantrell, "and I can disorganize you. The first to start past me gets a bullet. I'm through and so are you."

"Shoot the yellow-back!"

Cantrell's gun ripped from leather; a flat sheet of sound struck him in the face and all through him ran pain. He fell, massed shadows moved over him and the thunder of hoofs quaked in his ears, to diminsh and die. They had gone on, leaving behind the echo of Frawley's contemptuous words suspended in the chilling air: "The end of a double-crosser!" Cantrell's pony fiddled restlessly nearby.

"But they'll never make it now," gritted Cantrell. "All this noise has spotted them for the Y Cross patrol!" Knives sliced across his chest; a warm current of blood spread along his shirt front. One arm sank limply beneath him, but the other held, and in a sudden burst of strength he rolled against his horse, knowing there was only one sustained effort left in him. A kind of frenzy took hold and he never knew exactly how he reached the saddle, to sag there and sob for wind. Clinging to the horn, he used the pressure of his legs to swing the pony and presently felt the land slope upward, back to the rendezvous. Vitality leaked out of him and the sound and color of the night grew dimmer, but he was still canny enough to realize when he had reached the meeting point, and to turn north through the gulch. His thought was for water to curb the flames racing through his chest and stifling his breath. "If they want a trail," he thought grimly, "they got one, a yard wide and red as the sun." Vaguely he was aware of a fresher wind and the rousing detonations of gunfire below. Then those sounds dwindled and he took the change to be due to his own senses abandoning him; and it was like waking from a long sleep when he heard the soft trickle of water directly beside his horse. Lights flashed from somewhere. Letting go the horn, he fell into the tavern water trough. A great voice—it was Jastrow Brant's—yelled: "Lee Ann, bring the lantern!"

The water brought him directly back. Brant's big arms were holding him up and the full beam of the lantern blazed in his eyes; he saw Lee Ann's pallid face shining down.

"Never mind," he muttered. "I'm not in your house. This water's on a public road."

"Lift him!" cried Lee Ann. "They're coming up the trail now!"

"Not in the house," warned Cantrell. "It's Y Cross's night to howl and they'll be on your neck in a minute. I'm not asking for sympathy. Throw me off the road."

But Lee Ann's arm clung to his neck. "You're back—that's all I care about! You're back! You understand! Dad, lift him! Hurry!"

Jastrow Brant's arms were immense. They folded effortlessly about him and he felt himself swinging forward as in a cradle, dipping as the tavern keeper's game leg flinched against the ground. Presently he opened his eyes; he was in a chair by the fire and a pleasant peace ran through his body. A rider went by as on the van of storm wind, the heave of the pony's legs echoing into the house. Lee Ann was on her knees, both hands pressed against his body. "Close the door, Dad, close it!"

"Waste no grief on me," sighed Cantrell. "I'm not goin' to die. Throw me out and take care of yourself."

Lee Ann was crying again: "Close the door or they'll see him! They'll kill him!"

But Jastrow Brant, standing over Cantrell, stared down with a hard, black glance. "You've had your fling and what do you think of it now, mister outlaw?"

Cantrell's head rolled negatively. "Couldn't go through with it. Tried to stop 'em but they shot me down. A funny thing to live twenty-six years believin' yourself to be something you ain't. Can you imagine it—I've got a conscience!"

Lee Ann's grip tightened on Cantrell and he saw she was staring up at her father with bright, glowing eyes. "They'll never get him! Never! He's back to me!"

"For better or worse?" asked Cantrell, astonished at the humbleness in him.

"It will be better," said Lee Ann. "But if it must be worse—I'll share that too!"

86

Brant's hard eyes bored into Cantrell, probing, searching. "You got a bellyful, is that it? You've howled the last time on the hills?"

"I'm through, Brant. I couldn't do it. By this fire last night I saw somethin' I didn't dare destroy. Here, get rid of me. The pack's up the grade now."

Lee Ann stared at her father. "If you let them get him I'll never forgive it!"

Brant moved forward. His big arm reached up and brought down the blackened belt with its two suspended guns. He strapped the belt around him and Cantrell, watching closely, saw a different, harsher man standing in the room. Hoofs crushed across the yard and a trampling tide swept up the porch steps. Toomey and his men chocked the doorway. "Brant, I told yuh we was payin' off! I warned yuh to keep out of this! We want that man!"

Brant made a downward gesture with his arms and Toomey abruptly yelled, "Yo're wearin' yore guns!"

"My house is my castle, Toomey, and be damned to you! Get out of here!"

"Be careful, yo're buckin' the Y Cross," said Toomey, voice trailing into doubt.

"I've bucked bigger outfits in my day, Toomey. You see these guns—you know what I can do? Why you cream-faced rats, I slung lead afore you was dropped! Now get out of here before I make a shambles of this place!"

"I want no trouble with you, Brant," said Toomey. "But I got orders. You agree to promise—"

"I'm through," broke in Cantrell, drowsy and faint. "I hate your condemned outfit and some day I'll smash it. But not by the gun—not by the gun."

"That's all," said Toomey and backed away from the door. Brant wheeled about, still a flare and flicker of storm in the deep sockets. For a space he watched Cantrell, palms unconsciously caressing the belt cinched around him. "It's good sometimes," he finally muttered, "to have a bad name. My claws were cut many a year back but it's like tonic to know I once rode like a man—evil as the trail might have been. You know about me now, Cantrell?"

"The guns told me somethin'," admitted Cantrell.

"No man learns from advice. He's got to take the fall before he knows the hurt. I was like you. The wild bunch was my kind for a long while. But one night I made a ride too many. Your father—your own father, boy—smashed my hip with his shell in a runnin' fight. And when I come to my senses I thanked him for it. Tonight I'm only returnin' the favor of a good man. Hadn't that been so I'd of let you lay out there like a dog."

Cantrell made a motion toward his belt. "Hang up my gun with yours, Brant. Another lone wolf dies."

Lee Ann's fingertips brushed his face. "But not out in the hills and not alone."

Brant's face settled; the fresh, bold lines of revived outlawry died from his look. Unstrapping his belt he grunted to his daughter, "If you want him, Lee Ann, you better take care of him. Put him to bed and watch him close."

THE MISFIT

All day Ellen Prior worked with a fretful industry. She baked bread, cut up and fried four chickens, made a great batch of cookies, and had John Prior build a bonfire in the yard to cover a huge buried crock of beans which would simmer through the night. "If I only had a few bay leaves to put in. But there's never anything to do with in this forlorn country."

"There will be," said Prior.

"That's not now."

Long after Prior had finished his night chores she was still at her sewing and ironing.

He said, "We're only going twenty miles to Hardenburg's for a visit."

"We've not seen these people since November, and I'll not give any woman the chance to say we've not done as well as they."

"So we have," said Prioir. "We all got here poor, and nobody's had any chance to do better than anybody else this first winter. There's nothing in that to hurt your pride."

She went silently on with her work, but her silence argued with him.

They were away at daybreak in the big wagon which had brought them across the plains, the two matched gray oxen swaying under their yokes. Little Ben, still drowsy, crawled back to the bedding and curled on it to finish his sleep. They drove down the hill's incline to the meadow in which the winter wheat lay, skirted the point of land—Mrs. Prior's glance going to the fenced-in grave of her baby—and set out along the valley northward. She looked back to the cabin crouched beneath the great fire on the hillside and began to worry.

"Who'll take care of the animals?"

"One of Si Ree's squaws will come over tonight."

"Those creatures. I don't like them around, not even to touch the cow."

"You have got to take your neighbors as they come."

"I can't excuse sin," said Ellen Prior. "Suppose she steals something? Suppose she doesn't come, and the cow gets out?"

"Try to be easy about it. You're going for a visit."

"We've got so little," she said, "I couldn't bear to lose anything." She laid her hands across her lap, but they were restless. "It will be nice to see folks again. I'm so hungry for talk."

They crossed Cobway Creek's winter-roiled waters. This was February, an Oregon February, with the day moist and warm and half bright beneath ragged clusters of clouds. Gently the valley rolled forward, crisscrossed by willow-brushed streams and occasionally broken by low hills. The slow-going wagon crawled over a small rise and moved on through sodden meadows half green and half tawny. A mile behind them five people followed on horses.

"That's the Rands," said Prior.

Little Ben watched the Rands advance, and when he identified Susie Rand on one of the horses he dropped to the ground and waited for the family to come up—mother, father, two half-grown boys, and Susie. He jogged beside Susie Rand's pony.

Elton Rand said, "Climb up. It's a steady beast."

Susie reined in and took a foot from the stirrup. Little Ben, swung behind her, legs dangling and hands on the saddle cantle; his chin came to the top of her ash-colored hair. The quick-stepping horses overtook John Prior's lumbering wagon and the talk of the two families went back and forth as ringing explosions echoing across the empty land.

Elton Rand said, "What we doing at this meetin' outside of gettin' drunk on talk?"

"Raising a house for Wall Mecklin."

"He been here since November and no cabin yet? Sick man?"

"Lazy man," said Prior.

"Then let him rot in the rain."

Mrs. Prior said, "That would do for him, but he's got a wife and four children."

They stopped at noon to eat, and then went on through a soft land which subdued the sun into every gentle shade; and in the early afternoon other wagons and other riders began to show in the valley, they, too, swinging north. In the distance, Hardenburg's cabin began to stand up from the meadows, with a great many wagons around it.

Ellen Prior's voice carried the first unguarded warmth her husband had heard in it for a long while: "It will be good to see them again."

As soon as they reached the Hardenburg yard they were hailed by people they hadn't seen since the train's arrival in November, and Hardenburg called, "Just like night camp on the trail."

Prior stopped the wagon long enough to let his wife climb out, and he watched her throw her arms around Faith Potter; both women were crying. He swung his wagon beside another, neatly staggering it, and men moved over to lend him a hand with the unyoking—Dixon and Trevitt and Crabb and Brewster and Scott and all the others. He let the beasts move away toward Hardenburg's meadow.

"Now, then," said Dixon, "who draws night guard?"

"It all comes back, don't it?" said Prior.

He lighted his pipe and shook hands around, and was comforted to hear the old stories start again. The women made another group near the house, four months of frozen speech tumbling out. Ellen and Faith Potter were by themselves, their hands in lively motion as they talked, and Ellen was laughing, and brighter than Prior had seen her for a year.

The younger people were pairing already, and the children ran in and out of the parked wagons.

Hardenburg came over. He said, "I guess we might as well get to work. Where's Mecklin?"

Watt Irish murmured, "Sittin' in a patch of sun somewhere."

"Mecklin!"

"Wonder if his back's any better," said George Scott skeptically.

Mecklin came around Hardenburg's house and crossed toward the crowd at his own casual gait, slightly limping. John Prior's eyes took on a shade of austerity, for Mecklin had the air of a man who wished everybody to understand that none of this was any particular favor to him. He was a six-footer on the slim side, with granite-gray eyes and long black hair and a handsome face. He wasn't steady; he laughed or he swore and he claimed he had a temper which was a devil of a thing to control.

He came into the group and thrust his hands into his pockets; he tilted his head, looking down the length of his nose, and this gave him an uncivil appearance. "Who's so infernally anxious to see me?" He nodded at John Prior. "So you've come to help put me up a cabin. Would have done it myself long ago, but this damned back won't let me alone. You recall I got it at Fort Laramie, stepping off the wagon."

"No," said John Prior, "I don't recall." He searched Mecklin for bottom but found nothing he could like.

Mecklin curtly said, "Whether you do or don't, there's where it was."

"I didn't challenge the statement," said John Prior, his voice softer still. "I said I didn't recall."

Hardenburg said, "We've got part of the afternoon to cut logs. In the morning we'll lift the shebang and by one o'clock you'll all be on the road home. Who brought tools?"

Prior got saw and ax from his wagon, and discovered his wife with Mrs. Mecklin. The Christian pity would be rising in Ellen until nothing could stop it; for Rose Mecklin, once so pretty, was a worn-down, slatternly woman, shadowed by a sad look. John Prior fell in with the file of men passing across Hardenburg's meadow and watched Mecklin's biggest boy, a ten-year-old, rush up and catch his father's arm.

"Can I go?"

"There's only men. Now go back."

"Can I go?"

Mecklin wheeled, and the flat of his hand came through the air and caught the boy in the ribs and tumbled him away. "Dammit, do as I say! I won't be followed."

The short lines thickened around John Prior's eyes and his pipe bowl lifted to the increased pressure of his teeth. The party crossed a creek and stopped, at Hardenburg's suggestion. From the creek the land rose toward the fir-covered summit of a butte.

Mecklin said, "I want the cabin up that slope."

John Prior calculated the distance from cabin site to creek, and remembered the tired hands of Rose Mecklin. "Who's packing the water up the hill?"

"There's a spring near the top. I'll run a flume to the cabin."

"Before you get the flume built, who's packin' the water?"

Mecklin tilted his head to give Prior the suggestion of his ill-governed temper. John Prior answered the look steadily, until Mecklin retorted, "That's my problem, not yours," and turned away.

Prior continued up the hill to the timber. He faced a tree, sighted the place it ought to fall and began to chop, each stroke landing with a ringing wallop. He heard Mecklin giving orders: "I don't like these ten-foot cabins, boys. Make those front and back logs fifteen feet." Aggravation came out of John Prior's shoulders and went right into the ax blade.

Little Ben Prior rose from a wagon's shelter and raced in to declare himself free, beating Bob Mecklin by one long jump. Bob Mecklin said, "Not fair to hide in the wagons."

"Nobody said it wasn't," said little Ben. He stood like his father, feet flat on the ground and face on to young Mecklin. The other gave him a contemptuous push, but he remained stiff in his tracks, and finally young Mecklin turned to catch other victims. From the corner of his eyes little Ben watched Susie Rand walk idly over the yard, and he thrust his hands into his trousers and walked with the same indifference, not directly toward her but angling in and out of the wagon alleys until he came to her by the Trevitt wagon.

"Did you like my horse?" Susie asked. "It's a cayuse."

He said, "What's a cayuse?"

"That's Indian for horse."

She was not quite his height, though of the same age, and though he had known her four months he was never quite comfortable with the stone-gray inquisitivenss of her eyes. He walked away from the wagon, ignoring her; he heard nothing for a few moments, then suddenly she was beside him. She said, "Bob Mecklin's a year older than you are. He's ten."

"I'll be ten next year," he said, and felt humiliated.

"Then he'll be eleven."

He looked down at his feet slipping through the short meadow grass, thinking of no answer. The winter sun was a streak of light against the western hills, and the older men were returning from the butte. He wheeled toward the cook-fires rising in their yellow cones through twilight's beginning, and the smell of food was wonderful in the air. He stopped on the edge of the Hardenburgs' yard, and the moment he looked directly at Susie Rand she broke into a run and left him. He went on to the wagons and sat on a tongue, covertly watching her for a little while, and then he saw Bob Mecklin and he thought Bob was looking at him; half an anger and half a fear chased through him, one hot streak, one cold streak.

Rose Mecklin and her children were squatted around the

ground when John Prior came up with Mecklin. Mecklin didn't immediately sit down, but stared sharply at his wife. "I don't presume to intrude on other people. We've got grub and I've got a wife to fix it."

"If you were intruding," said Prior, "I'd tell you. Sit down."

It was Ellen's doing; she handed John Prior his plate, avoiding his eyes. Nothing did her soul so much good as to have this camp see that she had more than enough for her family and could feed guests; he noticed how her glance of seeming carelessness went to other fires, observing the food served elsewhere.

"You've done so well," said Rose Mecklin. "It just shows. I do miss milk for the children."

Mecklin flung a stinging intolerance at his wife. His voice used her hard: "If I don't provide well enough, say so."

"Oh, Wall, I'm not complaining." Fright fluttered over her, to tell John Prior how cowed she had been by this man.

"You do what you're supposed to do," said Mecklin, "and I'll do my part."

"I know—I know," she said uneasily.

"You don't know anything. Stop makin' me little in front of people."

"All right, Wall."

Mecklin stared insistently at her. The wish to hurt her was around his mouth: "I'll provide as well as any, when my back heals." He leaned on an elbow and his attention lifted to catch Carrie Gibson walking by; his glance followed her, covertly bold, warm in scheming. John Prior passed his cup to Ellen for refilling. He had lost the goodness of his supper, and little lines came about his eye sockets to give him a gaunt severity.

Around them the supper-fed and cheerful talk rose. Cass Rand had his fiddle going and a few folks began to sing. John Prior stuffed his pipe while the women did dishes, but he made no talk with Wall Mecklin, for there was a hardening disposition within him and outrage became a ball in his stomach.

Hardenburg drifted in to squat by the blaze, and in a little while other men settled around it. Rose Mecklin went away with her children, and women, one by one, walked toward the wagons. John Prior covertly observed his wife; she was drinking the goodness of this gathering as though it were cold and wonderful water.

In a moment everybody in the yard caught the tune Cass Rand played, all voices swelling through the night:

> *"Oh, Beulah Land, sweet Beulah Land,*
> *As on the highest mount I stand,*
> *I look away across the sea*
> *Where mansions are prepared for me . . ."*

His wife's face, suddenly and for only a moment, had on it the sweetness of a little girl's faith, and he lowered his eyes and looked upon his hard hands; when he raised his head she had gone to their wagon and the song was done.

"No work of his own," said Hardenburg, "but he'll get the best cabin in the valley. I wish I could find it funny."

Mecklin had left the group of men; he was farther down the yard, standing by Carrie Gibson in the circle of young people, making a fool of himself.

Prior asked, "What's the man living on?"

"It's the women," said George Dixon. "They give Rose Mecklin a little grub now and then. When Mecklin's not lookin', so's not to disturb his pride."

"I'd as soon let him go to hell," said Hardenburg.

"If he'd go alone," said George Dixon, "that would be fine. But he drags his family along. The cabin settles nothing and our work's for no good. He'll starve his family just the same."

"I gave him a job splittin' fence rails," said Watt Irish. "He did half a day's work and said his back wouldn't stand it."

Hardenburg said, "Well, what in thunder do we do with him?"

The group fell silent, struggling with their hard problem.

John Prior reached for his watch. "Ben," he called, and called only once, his voice carrying over the yard.

Little Ben drifted into the light-stained shadows behind the Hardenburg house. Bob Mecklin and the Quincy twins and Joe Irish sat in a circle, and Bob's voice, telling a ghost story, was pitched low. Little Ben stood near the circle and in a moment, without turning, he felt Susie Rand moving up behind him; she stopped at his elbow, and he grew cold and his stomach shivered, and the shiver went down his legs. She had said Bob was ten and he was only nine.

Bob bent forward and a deep "Whoo" came out of his throat, and he said, "That's the end of the story."

Little Ben spread his feet and stiffened them against the ground. He drew a long breath. "That's nothing," he said.

Bob Mecklin put both hands on the ground and rocked himself forward and rose, and stepped through the circle until he was close by little Ben; in the shadows he seemed taller than he had been in the afternoon. He said, "You want to fight?"

"I don't care," said little Ben.

Susie Rand was watching, and misery went through little Ben at the thought that he was showing fear. Bob Mecklin said, "I'll start it," and brushed a hand over little Ben's shoulder. Little Ben closed his eyes and struck with both hands; he jumped forward, his chin colliding with Bob's head. He wrapped his arms around Bob and carried him to the ground. He was hit in the stomach, and he rolled and jumped up, and found Bob in front of him again, and he put his head down and swung his fists wildly.

His hand hurt him; he opened his eyes and found Bob Mecklin sitting on the ground. His legs were shaking and he couldn't get enough wind into his lungs. He watched Bob Mecklin rise.

"Well, I guess that's the fight," said Bob, and started to walk away. Then he stopped and smiled half grudgingly. "You fight good."

Little Ben drew the back of a hand across his nose. A stinging ache increased around his mouth and he felt hollow.

Susie Rand said, "You knocked him down—you licked him."

"Did I?" he said. She stood still, she lifted a hand and touched his arm, and then he heard his father calling, and he left her. When he came to the fire his father looked at his bruised mouth.

John Prior said, "Time for bed," and watched his son go. He pulled apart the fire with his foot and said good night to Hardenburg, the last of the group to leave; and with his hands in his pockets he stood over the red coals, dreaming a little. Presently he strolled toward the meadow's edge, watching the stars; and his mind went out there until it could go no farther, and came back with its usual defeat. Directly behind him, in Mecklin's wagon, he heard the muffled sound of a woman weeping.

"Shut up," said Mecklin. "You're making me out a fool, making me out shiftless so everybody can see it."

The protest from Rose Mecklin was very small, but Prior heard her say, "Oh, Wall, people will hear."

"Shut up," said Mecklin. "It's your damned sad airs that have got 'em thinkin' wrong about me. I'm not goin' to have everyone lookin' down at me."

John Prior moved back to his own wagon, washed, and climbed over the wheel to where little Ben lay on the front tick. Prior said, "Well, who'd you fight?"

"Bob Mecklin."

"You stand up to him?"

"I knocked him down."

"Win or lose, I don't mind, just so you stand up to it. What was it about?"

"I don't know."

John Prior's chuckle was an easy suspiration in the blackness. "Good reason, and the usual one." He stepped to the rear of the wagon, undressed, and settled beside his wife. She was awake, waiting for him with something to say:

"You've got your grandfather's face, and it's cold as stone when something upsets you."

"I didn't mind the meal, but helping a man who'll not help himself is a bad thing."

"They've got to have a roof over their heads," she said.

"He's a fool, and making fools of us all."

"At least, the family will be warm," said Ellen.

"Poor stuff is poor stuff, and he'll use your pity for a crutch long as he lives."

"You want them to be cold, you want them to starve?"

He lay still, the strong feeling of Christian charity violated by the wrongness of this business. It was root hog or die, and Mecklin would not root, yet stayed fat at the expense of the neighborliness which none of them could escape. Prior was caught between the two extremes and found no answer. . . .

The wrongness was with him still in the morning as he walked over the meadow with the other men to resume work. The logs had been cut the previous afternoon, and Hardenburg, bringing over his oxen, snaked them down the butte to the cabin site. With twenty-five men on hand, all of whom had built their own cabins, it was no chore at all. A crew fell to notching and trimming, while others laid the logs in place. Dixon and Irish, both carpenters by trade, planed out boards for door and windows, and another set worked up shakes from a cedar.

Astraddle the ridgepole at ten o'clock that morning, John Prior bound in the rafters with rawhide and laid on the small poles to support the shakes. Down at the creek three men tramped dead grass and fern into a clay mudpile with their feet, and directly below Prior, in the cabin, Abel Burke and Tenno Jackson fashioned the fireplace, using this mud against a skeleton of poles.

Mecklin watched them as a straw boss would watch his crew, hands thrust into his pockets and hat raked back on his skull, "How thick you boys puttin' that mud on?"

"Thick enough," said Tenno Jackson.

"It don't look to me as though there's grass enough to bind

99

the clay." Mecklin left the cabin and took an adz and began an aimless chipping away at the ground by the door; he set aside the adz and descended the slope, standing by to watch the mudpile form. He straightened himself suddenly and put a hand at the small of his back, as though it had caught itself in a kink, and afterwards he settled on his haunches and stared across the valley.

Men came up to help John Prior lay on the shakes, and he, with his hands busy, watched women straggle across the meadow from Hardenburg's to see this new cabin; they made an admiring audience below him, their words striking into the warm day's quiet like silver splinters. Rose Mecklin walked into the cabin and came out, and she stood at a distance, with her soft face dreaming. It was a time when Mecklin ought to be with her, for this was a thing a man and wife did once in their lives; they might live in other cabins and build other houses, but this was the first and the best.

Prior looked around, and spotted Mecklin halfway down the slope, coming forward with Carrie Gibson, laughing and trying to make her laugh. She dropped a switch she carried in her hand, and Mecklin swiftly bent to lift it. John Prior's lids crept together as he saw that scene; there was nothing whatever wrong with Wall Mecklin's back.

Then the women went away, it drawing on toward lunchtime, and the last shakes were laid with pole battens lashed upon them, and the job was done. From his seat on the roof John Prior tried to feel the satisfaction of his labor, but could not.

Wall Mecklin's son came out of the cabin.

"Now go on," said Mecklin. "Back to your mother."

"Can't I stay?"

Wall Mecklin said, "Do what I tell you." He looked away from the boy, ignoring him, but the boy remained, and suddenly Mecklin wheeled and swung his hand hard across the boy's chest, tumbling him down the slope. "Do what I tell you," he said. . . .

John Prior slid from the roof to join the men standing

about. "She's a good one," said Hardenburg. "She's neat, she's tight, and she'll last a long time."

"She needs christenin'," said Wall Mecklin. "Where's that water bucket?"

John Prior stepped inside, walking the big room around. The smell of the cut fir and cedar was strong about him. He ran his hand along the log seams and stood before the wet-mudded fireplace; that would need a careful burning to dry tight and he doubted Mecklin had sense enough to do it. He lighted his pipe and turned about, and when he came into the doorway a full bucket of water, flung by Wall Mecklin, struck him straight upon the face and rushed down his clothes.

He took out his pipe and washed the water away with both hands; he heard Wall Mecklin's sharp explosion of laughter and saw the man standing with the empty bucket in his hand, amusement glittering in his eyes. "Well, Prior, you get christened with the house."

Prior thrust the pipe into his pocket. He looked around and saw no amusement anywhere else, and he stared at Wall Mecklin until the man's laughter faded. Mecklin lifted his chin to sight down his nose, the snaky look of arrogance coming. He said, "Dammit, you stepped into it. I have never apologized to any living thing, and I don't propose to start now."

Prior stepped gravely forward and delivered one massive blow direct to that narrow face. The bucket which had been in Mecklin's fist went bounding down the hill, and Mecklin fell backward full length and began to roll, to scramble, to tear himself off the earth. John Prior might have been done with him then, but Mecklin slid a hand toward his hip pocket as though to draw a gun. The falseness of the threat renewed Prior's rage; he rushed on, struck Mecklin again, knocked him down, and watched him tumble the rest of the way to the creek, landing on hands and knees at the water's edge.

Prior's long legs jumped over the distance. He seized Mecklin at neck and crotch, raised him a full four feet from the ground, and dashed him into the water and turned back up the slope. He was talking within himself, not a sound coming from him; the righteous rage was a tide rushing back and forth, and a mighty wind blew through him. He reached the cabin's yard, embarrassed by what he had done, yet still controlled by his wrath.

"That's a good end to it," said Hardenburg.

Mecklin rose from the creek and stopped to look at himself, to shake the water from his clothes. He lifted his eyes toward the crowd, his face stiff and yet without the insolence which Prior had so often seen there; then he stared across the meadow toward Hardenburg's house, and John Prior thought, "Now he's going to run from it. A rotten apple's always rotten and nothing can be done about it." He was greatly surprised, therefore, when Mecklin moved up the slope and faced the crowd.

Mecklin looked straight at him. "What have you got against me? What've you always had against me—you and all the rest?"

John Prior found himself distantly respecting Mecklin for a quality he had not believed the man owned; but there was still anger enough within him to make him blunt: "You're a fool in your head and no good to your family. You're a clown to the women, they laugh at you behind your back. You're a joke to every man here, for you've dragged your feet and you won't work. If it weren't for your wife and kids you could starve and be dammed to you. It won't do."

Mecklin looked about him; his eyes searched each man in the crowd, with a strange, frozen care. He looked back to Prior, and he said in a very low voice, "I have not felt I was one of you, gentlemen, and it's not been an agreeable thing to bear."

Prior was strongly troubled, and he looked across the meadow to be sure that Mecklin's son had seen none of this; and he began to dislike himself. "Well," he said, still blunt, "we've got a long time to live together, all of us, and it's best to live together agreeably."

"What you want me to do?" said Mecklin.

"You've got to take care of your family. Now, Irish wants rails and so do I, and you ought to be able to do your hundred a day in return for grub in rain, snow, or sun. Sick or well, you ought to be able to do a day's labor and make no fuss about it. And when harvest's come, you ought to be as well off as the rest, if it's in your make-up to sweat."

Mecklin looked thoughtfully to the ground, and for a little while John Prior's old doubts had their way and he expected nothing. Then Mecklin's chin rose and he stared directly at Prior, and he quietly said, "Very well," and turned down the hill.

Hardenburg murmured, "Do you believe it, John?"

"I think it's best to believe, until he shows us to be wrong."

"And makes fools of us again?"

"Well," said Prior, "if we preach religion to him we had better exercise some ourselves. I will risk being a fool."

All the wagons were hitched and a farewell calling went around the yard, very cheerful. John Prior watched his wife take both Faith Potter's hands, smile, and turn to the wagon. He gave her a boost to the seat and took his place, and spoke the oxen into motion. The calling went on, farther and farther reaching as the wagons rolled apart, and in Hardenburg's yard a few last, loitering people were singing.

He didn't look directly at his wife's face, but he knew she was at peace, for her hands were softly folded and at rest, and peace came from her as a fragrance. She drew a long sigh. "It was so good," she said.

He spoke to the off-ox and checked its swinging, and looked back to see little Ben framed at the tail gate.

Ellen Prior said, "How'd Mecklin get his bruised face?"

"A log," said Prior.

"It will come out all right," she said, her voice gentle.

"It may be," said Prior. He was serene, for he, too, had

103

been hungry for talk, and the gathering had been as a strong meal nourishing him. Then he saw his wife's hands lightly stir, and he knew her idleness was done with.

"It's such a long time to leave stock, and the skunks have been bad lately. I don't trust those squaws much, Prior, and just these two days of visiting have piled up such a lot of work."

He sat back on the seat, inwardly smiling. "I know," he said, "but it's all right."

"That will do to say," she said firmly. "But it's not words that get work done."

From the tail gate little Ben watched the Rand's come forward, the quick-stepping horses soon drawing abreast the wagon. He dropped his head, then lifted it and found Susie Rand's eyes on him as though he were a stranger. He looked away indifferently, and the family passed on. Presently he turned his head again, and saw Susie Rand suddenly swing her body and throw a smile at him. After the Rands were well ahead, he jumped to the ground and walked beside the wagon, following the girl with his glance until she grew small in the distance.

DEEP WINTER

One night the snow came, drifting soundless out of a sky that lay gray and close upon Ingrid settlement and the four hundred homesteaders scattered across the flats. By the fourth morning all fence lines were dark wrinkles dimly showing on the snow's crust, and four-foot drifts lay against homestead shanties. Breaking road between his quarter section and Ingrid, Tom Kertcher noticed how straight the smoke rose from shanty chimneys, through the very thin air.

He had mounted a wagon bed on homemade sled runners and had fashioned a sort of leathern snowshoe for his horses; even so the going was labored, the horses now and then plunging into the snow's soft spots.

He came into Ingrid, passed Mrs. Rand's hotel and Solomon's store, and drew up before Brewerton's blacksmith shop and house. Letty Brewerton had seen him approaching and was at the shanty door, smiling at him. Kertcher said, "Sort of an American Siberia," and got off the seat. He was plain and solid, an easy and practical man with coal-black hair above a strong nose and mouth, and not much of a hand to give his feelings away. But when he looked at her she saw how pleased he was to be with her—there was that unreserved approval in his eyes. "I'm breaking road," he said. "Maybe you'd like to go for a ride."

She said, "Wait until I get my coat," and disappeared. Brewerton, Letty's father, worked in the adjoining shed, the sound of his blacksmith hammer very harsh in the thin air. Letty's mother appeared at the doorway to say a few words.

Kertcher said, "Likely to have a norther. You have plenty of wood?"

"It is piled beyond the shop," said Mrs. Brewerton.

"Not close enough. In a real blizzard you couldn't walk that far."

Letty came out and stepped into the sled and he tucked a blanket around her. Mrs. Brewerton called, "Keep warm, Letty," and cast a curious glance at them as they drove away, never quite certain how things were between these two.

Letty said, "Miss me?"

"Four days is a long time."

"That's nice," she murmured. She bent her shoulder so that it touched Kertcher and thus they drove along the road, two calm and reticent people who had reached some kind of an understanding without ever speaking of it. They passed Swenson's house at the junction of the schoolhouse road; they continued south, coming by Ben Lowe's place— a small shack and attached tent, housing Lowe and his wife and four children. A mound of snow in the yard indicated where Lowe, the most shiftless of men, had left his plow and cultivator to rust away. Letty said, "I don't think they've much wood or food."

"He sat around all fall, cryin' about hard luck when everybody else worked."

"I can't think of his family being hungry."

"Put him in the middle of a store and he'd be too lazy to reach up to a shelf."

They moved on, following the first ruts cut by Kertcher and, five miles from Ingrid, they turned into Kertcher's quarter section and stopped before the shanty.

He sat still for a moment, staring straight before him. He said slowly, "If I take you into the house, Letty, I'll kiss you—and maybe we shouldn't be hiding a thing like that behind four walls." He turned to her, drew her against him and looked down at her so that she saw the sharp angles of his heavy mouth. She lifted her head and knew she provoked

106

him into the kiss and was glad of it; she was smiling when she pulled away from him and got out of the sled and waited for him to open the door.

He had built larger than most homesteaders, and he had built with more care. The house had three rooms, all of them sealed in with finish lumber. A rear door led to a shed which was filled with wood. Beyond the shed was a small lean-to barn.

She knew the house had been built for her; it was one of those unsaid things between them. But she also knew he would not ask her to marry him until fall had come and he had put away his first crop as a demonstration that he was able to provide for her. He was that way. But when she thought of how close they were, and how many good days they were missing, and of how much she could do for him, she had an instant when she wanted to cry.

She looked at him and he saw something of what she felt, for he drew a long breath. "We'd better get out of here before I—"

"Why shouldn't you?"

For a moment they stood staring at each other. Presently he dropped his eyes. "I think," he said, "we ought to start back." Once more on the sleigh seat, he paused to fill and light his pipe and he led the talk to safer ground. "Dirty weather coming. I wish the people on the flats had better shelter."

Going back down the road, her own thoughts still confused, she realized how natural it was for him to worry about the homesteaders; he had a streak of responsibility in him that people felt, and because of that he had come to be somewhat of a leader on the flat, without his asking. They followed the ruts of their previous trip as far as the Lowe shanty, and turned into the yard.

Mrs. Lowe opened the door for them, a heavy, shapeless woman—unkempt and complaining. She made an ineffectual swipe at her hair and invited them in, using half of the same breath to condemn the weather. "Nobody can do anything. It ain't any use even to try. We've all got chills."

The four children, from three to nine, were underfoot in the single room of the shanty and the place was in complete confusion. A stove and table crowded one side, a bed occupied most of the other, and Lowe lay covered with quilts on the bed, smoking his pipe. A doorway without a door led into a tent which formed the second room. Mrs. Lowe's eyes saw at once that both Letty and Kertcher were unfavorably impressed with Lowe's idleness and she sprang to her husband's defense. "He ain't been well all fall. He never got over a sprain to his back durin' the summer."

"You ought to put a door against that tent," said Kertcher. "You're burnin' wood to heat the whole outside world."

"I'll get to it," said Lowe and seemed contented enough with his pipe.

Letty's quick glance meanwhile noted the cupboard and saw nothing much in the line of food. She turned to the door with Tom Kertcher, speaking casually to Mrs. Lowe:

"There's always a few neighbors in at Mrs. Rand's during the evenings. Come over."

"If I can get my chores done we may come," said Lowe.

Kertcher spoke with an irritated disgust when they drove away: "Too lazy to get up and walk half a mile to get his kids warm."

Coming into the hotel that evening, Kertcher found the usual roundabout group gathered—the Brewertons, Mrs. Rand and her daughter Tara, old Solomon who had recently built the store, the Swensons, and Judith Prescott, the teacher who boarded with them. The Jacksons had come in from the schoolhouse section, riding with Curtis Kilrain and Elizabeth Marsh. Andy Pierce had made the trip from his Oxhead ranch and Charley Graves was just in with mail from Virgil, five hours late on the trip, bringing the sheriff with him. The Lowes came in with their children shortly after Kertcher arrived.

The sheriff, going his rounds of duty with an eye for new

friends as well, was an excellent storyteller, and the sharpness of the weather put everybody in excellent spirits. The men more or less grouped together while the ladies went into the kitchen to help Mrs. Rand, who presently came out with a tray of sandwiches and a pot of coffee. Kertcher noticed that Letty made a point of serving the Lowe youngsters; and he noticed too, how Ben Lowe's eyes came over to observe that. When Letty offered Lowe a sandwich, he refused it. "Just ate—not hungry," he said. The man was lying, of course, yet Kertcher saw something in Lowe then he had not seen before, which was pride. Meanwhile, the talk went on, weather and crops and roads and politics and babies. During the tag end of the evening the sheriff drew Kertcher aside.

"I can't cover all this county," he said. "Should be a deputy down here. It's only worth thirty a month, but among you homesteaders that's helpful money. I thought of you, naturally."

"I don't need it."

"Then I give you the disposal of the job," said the sheriff. "You pick the man."

"I'll get you somebody," Kertcher said.

"Done," said the sheriff, and moved toward the ladies, having some sort of a word for each of them. The Lowes, late arrived, were first to go; and as they moved toward the door Kertcher caught an expression from Letty. She came by him, murmuring, "Give him some kind of work, Tom."

Being a hard-laboring man, Kertcher had no stomach for the suggestion. Nevertheless he walked toward the doorway, stopping Lowe. "Ben," he said, "I could use some help tomorrow. I've got some timbers to fit in the barn."

Lowe studied it. "I got a lot of chores of my own," he said, "but maybe I can do it for you."

He walked into the night, leaving the plain intimation that it was he who conferred the favor.

Kertcher expected Lowe by eight in the morning, but it was beyond nine when the man showed up in the barn. "Long walk," he explained, "and I had some chores to do

109

first." He was prepared to spend another half-hour in conversation, but Kertcher gave him an adz and set him to the chore of dubbing the end of a six-by-six timber; all this was indoor work, in preparation for springtime when the barn frame would be lifted into place. Promptly at noon, Lowe dropped the adz and followed Kertcher into the house, sitting by while Kertcher turned out a bachelor's meal. There was no end to the man's self-esteem or his assurance. He had a firm opinion on any subject; and one by one he brought these subjects up, settled them and went on to another. At one, they returned to work; at four o'clock Kertcher said, "That'll be all, Ben," and found three dollars in his pocket.

His temper was sorely strained by the manner in which Lowe accepted the money. "I've made better wages, Kertcher—but if that's all you feel you can give I won't argue."

"Fine," said Kertcher, and watched Lowe depart. The man, he thought, had no knowledge of his own failure.

The following morning was biting cold, and the air had an extreme thinness, but the woolly clouds remained low, obscuring that monument of outlawry half a mile across the river, Brazil Mullan's long cabin and barn. Kertcher thought, "Storm around the corner," and spent half a day bringing water up from the river, two buckets at a time. He cooked himself a noon meal and began to think of his neighbors, most of whom were city people with no knowledge of real bad weather; and around three o'clock he hitched and started for Ingrid. He dropped a warning at Swenson's and touched as far as the Jackson place. There was a dull streak in the north and the air, damp as it was, had an electric feel. When he got as far as Mrs. Rand's he observed Ben Lowe coming from the back of the hotel. "Ben," he said, "watch out. Storm coming."

"Been through a lot of them," said Lowe and moved homeward.

Kertcher noticed both Harriet Rand and Letty at the back door, and left his sled to join them. There was a pile of wood scattered around the doorway, recently chopped. Mrs. Rand said uncertainly, "Is that as much as a man should chop in a day?"

Kertcher said, "You hired him to do this? How much did you pay him?"

"Four dollars," said Mrs. Rand. "Was that about right? He needed the work."

Kertcher studied the pile of wood, holding himself strictly under control. "Harriet," he said, very quietly, "better to feed him outright than be bilked like this."

"He has pride," said Letty. "He wouldn't stand charity."

"He'll stand that before he'll stand starving," said Kertcher. He thought of his original purpose in coming here, warned the two women of the storm and turned back to his sled. He caught up with Lowe at the latter's front door.

"Ben," he said, " you figure that a day's work you did for Mrs. Rand?"

Lowe gave him an affronted glance. "She didn't have to hire me."

"Well," said Kertcher, "that's pure gall. You sting a woman who's as hard up as you are and then you stand there and say it was her fault. What's the matter with your mind?"

Mrs. Lowe flung open the door and stood behind her husband. "You stop talking like that to my husband, Tom Kertcher!"

Lowe reached around with an arm and pushed his wife into the house. He reared up and tossed his shoulders back. "If that's the way you people think about a few stinkin' dollars—" he yelled, and clawed his pocket, brought out the four silver pieces and flung them into the snow. He shouted, "I don't need the dirty stuff!" and wheeled into the house.

Tom Kertcher went down the road, half ashamed of himself. He thought, "Darned fool really believes he's a big man stoopin' to small chores." He looked back, and at the moment saw Mrs. Lowe on her hands and knees in the snow digging for the money Lowe had thrown away.

Mrs. Lowe found three of the four dollars and went back into the house. "Ben, you shouldn't of done that," she said. "We won't find the other dollar until spring."

He had put himself on the bed; he lighted his pipe and slapped out the spilled tobacco burning against his clothes. "She didn't have to hire me."

"We need the money," said Mrs. Lowe in her complaining voice. She lighted a lamp and set about dinner. The young ones played around the cramped quarters, behind the stove and under the bed.

"Pete," said Lowe to the nine-year-old, "go bring some wood into the tent."

"Never mind," said Mrs. Lowe, "I'll do it myself later. Come on to supper."

He got up, moved two paces and sat down at the table, the youngsters crowding around him, Mrs. Lowe standing. The meal was bacon, beans and coffee; even the youngest one had his share of the coffee. Lowe ate what he wanted, and drank his coffee and lay back on the bed smoking. "Libby, help your ma with the dishes."

"Libby, go to bed," said Mrs. Lowe. "I can't be wipin' your nose all winter."

Lowe watched Libby go through the blank doorway into the tent. He said, "I'll put up a door tomorrow. Maybe bank a wall of snow all around the tent. That'll be warm—way the Eskimos live."

"Don't hurry about it," said Mrs. Lowe. "Spring's only four months away."

She finished the dishes, chased the children to bed and undressed by the stove. She fed the stove a last time, turned the damper not quite shut and blew out the light. The weight of her body, when she settled into bed, lifted Lowe's side a full six inches. He got up and took off his shoes and pants and shirt; he sat crouched on the bed's edge, smoking his pipe in the dark. "I always had a fine pen hand. I could put Solomon's books in fine shape. Or I could run for sheriff. I could beat that fellow. I'm the only man with an education around here."

She reached out with a rough but affectionate arm and pulled him flat. "Get under the covers, you fool."

He ate his cornmeal and drank his coffee at breakfast. He went outside and circled the house. He yelled, "Pete, bring in some wood for your mother," and came back to the kitchen. Mrs. Lowe said, "Keep out of my way this mornin'. I got to wash."

He stood still in the front room, watching her. "Emma, he said, "you think that's what people think about me?"

"I know all your old tunes, Lowe. Don't start no new ones and upset me."

He got his rifle and sat on the bed and oiled it; he put four cartridges into his pocket and struggled into his big coat. Mrs. Lowe gave him a sharp look. "What you got on your mind now?"

"I hear there's antelope down by the river."

"Ah," she scoffed, "you couldn't hit a barn."

"But," he said, "I can provide for my family. They can't say I can't." He went out the door and slammed it behind him.

Kertcher stood in the yard and studied the morning sky and saw the sheet of blackness in the north; the wind, also from the north, would be bringing that blackness on. The air was perfectly still, and as thin as he could ever remember it being. Turning into the barn, he hitched the sled and threw in such rope as he could find and drove it to the front yard. He got all his blankets off the bed, he put on an extra shirt and an extra pair of socks; he took a bottle of whisky from the cupboard and he slid a compass into his pocket and started for Ingrid.

All of the homestead shanties were flimsy enough, but some of them were so loosely thrown together that a seventy-mile wind would tear them apart unless they were guyed to the ground; and that meant a family wiped out within half an hour of exposure. He turned immediately east. He

113

stopped at Pilkington's, Rath's and McCory's, saying the same thing each time: "Real blizzard coming. Pile wood up against the side of your house for an anchor. Get some water inside in case your chimney catches fire. If you burn out you're helpless. Don't try to go anywhere once it hits. You couldn't walk a straight line and you couldn't see. Warn your nearest neighbor."

He circled Charley Mortlett's place, a mile east of the school, and went on to Parch Cobbin's, with the black wall of weather bearing down fast.

"Get your place tied down," he called to Cobbin, and headed for Ben Lowe's.

Half a mile from Cobbin's, he felt a warning breath of wind; and then the silence broke and he heard the distant rumbling and sighing and shrilling of the blizzard. He had the horses pointed straight upon the small vague shape of the Lowe shanty; in the semidarkness closing around him he took out his compass and got his bearings on the Lowe place. Half a minute later he looked up to see something lift and sail like a giant piece of paper through the sky. It was the Lowes' tent.

The horses veered from the wind and in one great transition from half-light to smothered dark, the Lowe shanty faded from sight. He was then less than a quarter-mile from his target, and by instinct he pulled the team constantly to the north, but even so, when he looked at his compass he found he had drifted. He said to himself, "Bad night," and listened to the words rip away from his mouth. "If I miss the place—" He caught it as a shadow on his right and swung the sled hard by the door. He yelled at the door and saw Mrs. Lowe open it. He said, "Get in!"

She was a shapeless, frightened woman with her hair blowing over her face, her children crowded close around her. "Lowe's gone! I got to stay and keep a light burnin'!"

He jumped from the sled and seized the children one by one. He pulled at the reluctant woman, one eye constantly on the restless horses. "Your house won't be here in half an hour!"

114

She fought with him and she began to cry. "I told him not to go! He'll die!" When he drove away he had to hold her from jumping out. She was a big, loose woman and hard to hold; so that he finally had to beat her will down with strong language: "Don't be a fool! You want the kids to die?"

He pulled the team into the drive of the blizzard and held them into it, searching for Ingrid's lights. He tried his compass again and saw the vague swinging of the needle. He heard Mrs. Lowe cry something at him and afterward she climbed back into the wagon box with the children. Forward he thought he saw a wisp of a gleam to the left, and the sled runners grated over some kind of metal. He turned left, caught the light a second time and used it for a beacon, drawing up before Mrs. Rand's hotel. Lowe's wife climbed out with her children and hurried inside. Kertcher swung the team between the hotel and the store and beat his way back to the hotel.

Half the settlement had collected here and Mrs. Lowe was crying out her story, her big face homely with despair: "Lowe's gone—"

Kertcher said, "When did he leave—which way did he go?"

"Nine o'clock. He said there was antelope by the river."

Andy Pierce and Charley Graves, both cowmen who knew the country well, gave Kertcher grave glances.

"He'd follow the road," surmised Kertcher, "because it is easier walkin'. He might have smelled trouble and ducked into my house."

Andy Pierce used that as reassurance for Mrs. Lowe. "Sure he did."

But Kertcher doubted it. He drew Pierce and Graves aside. "The fool's lost. I've got to go look."

"Don't be a sucker," said Pierce. "It'll blow your scalp off in another two hours."

"I can get as far as my place," said Kertcher. "Might find him on the road. He'll walk until he's all done in and he'll drop."

"Thin chance. How you goin' to get home?" Pierce asked.

"Wind at my back. Five miles exactly. Straight south and use a compass."

"That's two men dead instead of one. I'm telling you."

Charley Graves said, "Half an hour out in that stuff and you'll lose the ability to calculate distance. On top of that your horses may refuse to face the weather."

Mrs. Lowe saw them standing together. She searched them with her eyes and seemed to see an answer, for suddenly she spoke at them in a dull, small voice: "I know what you think of him. But he's my man, isn't he?"

Nobody said a word. Kertcher looked at her and suddenly he smiled at her and turned toward the door. Pierce and Graves followed him and Letty Brewerton said, "Wait," and came up to him. There was a kind of hardness on her face, made by fear. She wanted to hold him back, she wanted to tell him of her fear. But all she said was: "Are you warm enough, Tom?"

"Yes," he said, and smiled again.

Charley Graves said, "Longer we wait the thicker it gets."

"Who's we?" asked Kertcher, and then noticed that Charley had borrowed Pierce's huge buffalo coat.

"Two fools are better than one," said Charley. When he opened the door a great wind and a great crying rushed in. The two men bent against it, closed the door and beat their way to the sled and team parked between the two buildings. The wind's terrible force keeled both men on the seat when they swung out of that shelter and turned south. Charley Graves yelled, "Now, ain't this silly?" For a moment Kertcher saw Mrs. Rand's hotel lights dancing in the flitter of snow; twenty feet onward he looked back and saw only blackness. Charley Graves shouted: "Keep the wind centered on your tail bone—that's north kickin' at you."

The storm was a hard, steady push on Kertcher's shoulders. When he turned his head, wind drove breath into his nostrils, making him open his mouth to catch air, and the drive of snow stung his cheeks like small buckshot. It was, he guessed, two o'clock in the afternoon with the blizzard's darkness pressing down and the tumult of the blizzard making its wild, polar confusion all around him. He tried to sight Lee Gantry's shanty, slightly short of the schoolhouse turn-off, and found nothing; and then, looking upon the smothered blankness in front of him he felt the complete futility of seeking one man in a blind area of perhaps fifty square miles.

Charley Graves cried, "That big off mare of yours has got a longer reach than the other mare! Pulls you to the left!" Kertcher felt a sharper bite on his left cheek and headed the team rightward. The sled's runners scraped metal and bumped against wood. "Fence!" whooped Graves. "Still on the road!"

Kertcher bent over to take the pressure from his shoulders. He had a scarf wound around his face, but the wind got beneath it and crashed into his ears. Working with the wind in this manner he felt as though team and sled were coasting down a steady hill and the feeling tricked his judgment of distance. The horses were going at a boosted walk, better than three miles an hour, at which rate he should reach his shanty in about an hour and a half. He pulled out his watch and handed it to Charley. "We left Brewerton's at ten minutes of two. What time now?"

Graves put his nose against the watch. He held it a long while. "Looks like a quarter after. Don't seem that long. You're swingin' left again!"

Kertcher pulled right. Snow began to build up a drift in the fore part of the wagon box, chilling his feet. He stamped his feet and he thought of Ben Lowe, visualizing the man's heavy, self-satisfied face; and irritation built a heat in him. The sled runners sent back a different sound and the horses fiddled as they walked. "What's that?" yelled Charley Graves.

Kertcher stopped the team, and Charley Graves cautiously left the sled. There was a steady crying roar over Kertcher's head, a vast dismal yell coming out of upper

117

emptiness. He boxed his hands together and felt coldness move through his clothes and through his bones, like on-coming sleep. Charley Graves came back. "Somethin' on the snow, like canvas! Petered out in my direction!"

Kertcher handed over the reins and went off his side of the sled. He dug his feet into something half solid and he got down and crawled; he struck a rope and he sat still a moment, trying to figure it, and then remembered Lowe's tent that had blown away. He turned back at a slightly dif-ferent angle, still crawling, and reached a rolled-up section of the tent; something gave beneath him and something moved. He dug into the roll, found a loose edge and put his head beneath it. A hand came up and struck him across the face and a voice said: "Who's that?" That was Lowe's voice. Then Lowe said: "Pull down that edge—you're lettin' cold air in."

Kertcher stood up and jerked the covering away, bringing Lowe to his feet, vague in the black. Kertcher pushed the man onward toward the sled. He yelled at Charley Graves: "Here's Lowe! Drive up a few feet!"

He heard Charley Graves' cussed-out astonishment as he drove the team on; Kertcher turned back, intending to salvage the tent, but as he dropped to his knees the wind lifted the canvas and he saw it lift into the air, like a giant bat, and vanish. He crawled back to the sled and took the reins. The wind had gotten thoroughly into him and he was chilled through and began to shake; when he swung the sled around into the full beat of the blizzard he felt a kind of strained rigidness in his muscles. He knew then all three of them were in danger.

Lowe crouched in the wagon bed behind Kertcher's back. Lowe yelled: "Mighty foolish thing for you to do! I was warm in that tent! I could of stayed there all week!"

Kertcher restrained his answer; he heard Charley Graves yell back at Lowe: "How the hell did you find the tent?"

"It just sailed through the air at me! I grabbed it and rolled into it!"

"The Lord sure protects some people!" howled Charley.

118

"No use my gettin' cold!" said Lowe. "I'm goin' to roll up in the blankets!"

The blast was hard to take, but Kertcher had to keep it directly against him to be sure he was traveling north. When he felt the force of it drop off from one side of his face he knew he was veering and pulled the reluctant team around. In this blackness it was impossible to read the compass.

"See anything?" yelled Charley Graves. "My eyes are full of ice!"

"No!"

The snow whipped against him, knifelike as it struck his exposed face, and sleet formed on his eyebrows. He stamped on the wagon bed to bring feeling back to his dead feet. There was never a moment when he didn't have to wrestle the horses back into the wind; they were taking a beating and they didn't like it. He got to thinking of how small a target Ingrid was—just a spot a hundred feet wide in a hundred-mile distance—and felt the runners scrape across metal again.

"Road fence!" said Charley Graves. "We're on the track!"

He wasn't sure. The constant flicker of mealy snow threw his vision off; it gave him a feeling of unbalance, and the constant rush and roar of the wind disturbed his judgment. He had, he realized, lost his sense of direction completely. That was probably why so many men died when they got caught in a thing like this. He thought he saw the shadow of a shanty on his left and he pulled over and found it only an illusion. He straightened again, but he felt the growing weakness of the horses. If they stalled on him there was only one thing left—tip over the wagon box and crawl beneath it with the blankets and hope to live out the storm. It wasn't much of a chance.

The horses stopped and refused to go straight on, as much as he urged them. He hauled them half around, and got them started, but Charley Graves called, "Wait!" and slipped from the sled, disappearing. When he came back he yelled,

"That was the big survey post! We've overshot Ingrid! Turn left! Half a mile to go! Feelin' a little cool?"

"Sleepy!"

Charley Graves hit him a heavy blow on the back. "Wrong place to sleep!"

The horses were halfheartedly pulling; wind carried them sidewise steadily, so that Kertcher was pointing them back at every short distance. He closed his eyes to visualize the movement of the sled across that half-mile; far off he heard a sound, and then he felt a great wallop on his back, and opened his eyes to hear Charley Graves speaking: "I think there's a light off to the right."

He looked and saw no light; the constant lacing of the snow made a thousand vague points that looked like distant flashes. But he pulled to the right, and stood up to slash the rein ends down on the horses; they stopped on him and then he realized the wind no longer blew against him. It was a howling behind him and a roar ahead of him but here in this spot was a strange calm. "Must be losing my head," he thought. He gave the reins to Charley Graves, left the sled and walked straight into the black side of a building. He stood against it and he yelled; he pounded his fist against the building. A door came open and he saw Brewerton in the light—Brewerton and Pierce and other people suddenly behind these two. It occurred to him then that the team had cut a complete circle around Ingrid and had drifted between the hotel and Solomon's store.

Graves and Ben Lowe came up. Brewerton said, "I'll take the team. You get in the house."

"Wait," said Graves. He bent and caught a handful of snow. He shoved it against Kertcher's face. "Feel that?"

"Yes."

"Then we can go in," said Charley. Ben Lowe had gone ahead of them, lugging something in his arms. When Kertcher got into Mrs. Rand's kitchen he found the settlement group gathered there and he saw Ben Lowe standing before his wife, with a quarter of beef. Lowe said, "Here's some meat, Mama."

` There wasn't a word in the room. Lowe's wife looked at him, long and straight and affectionate and it seemed to Kertcher she was a younger woman than he had guessed her to be. She said softly, "Put that down, Lowe," and when he put it down she threw out her heavy arms and hugged him. "You're a fool," she said. "Such a terrible big fool. You caused so much trouble."

Lowe said, "I'm all right." He gave Kertcher and Graves a self-assured grin. "I'm warmer than those fellows. Think I can stand weather better than they can. Foolish of them to come after me. I was comfortable and in no trouble at all."

Charley Graves had been studying the quarter of beef. "Where'd you get that?"

"Shot it," said Lowe, and grinned at Charley Graves' shocked face. "But that's all right, too. I got to thinkin'. Here's people hungry and there's Brazil Mullan across the river—a thief and a rustler eatin' well off beef that ain't his. So I went over and shot one of his cows. He heard the shot and came out with a couple of men, but I drove them back just when the storm broke." He had an audience. And he felt big about it; he was the same old Lowe again and he spoke to Kertcher with his egotism beginning to show: "I don't know why people should be afraid of that crowd. I'd take my chances against 'em any day." Having said it he took his wife's arm and moved on into the big room.

He left a relieved and exasperated group behind him. Charley Graves shook his head, repeating a former observation: "The Lord sure protects some people."

"Well," said Kertcher, "he believes he's as tough as Mullan —and I sort of think he means it. He's no good for some things but for some things he might do well—particularly the kind of a thing in which he feels big, and has to live up to it." He grinned at Charley Graves, at Andy Pierce. "There's your deputy sheriff. The thirty a month will keep him from starvin' and I believe he'll do all right."

Letty was near him, watching him; and now he looked at her and forgot there was anybody else in the kitchen. But the others understood about this and somebody started for the big room so that presently Letty and Kertcher stood alone. He had some trouble getting his pipe out of his pocket because of the stiffness of his hands. He packed and lighted it and the smoke burned his wind-blistered skin. Letty stepped nearer him, looking up with her sweet, grave expression. He saw the warmth in her eyes and he felt the warmth of her voice:

"A little bit cold outside, Tom?"

"Somewhat chilly."

That was the end of it, neither of them being of the talkative kind. He pulled his pipe down, cast a quick glance at the doorway, and bent and kissed her.

PRIDE

The four crisp hoof-prints came suddenly off the right ridge into the road where Matt Tavener, riding for Sundown from his Turkey Track ranch, found and followed them toward the Sixes River bridge ahead. There had been a mist during the night and the impressions were quite clear, cut in by very small shoes with worn cleats. Meanwhile the rain, impounded in a sullen sky throughout the day, was beginning; straight and heavy-bodied and almost silent. When he reached the bridge his slicker was adrip and he was thinking the burnt August range would be needing this water, but after that he stopped, rouséd by something turned from commonplace to strange. The tracks wheeled short of the bridge and went along the southern margin of the river, soon fading under the dusk.

Matt Tavener's long torso swooped down. Gone alert, he said, "What for?" It was like a signal thrown in his face and his answer was immediately to swing and go beside those tracks a quarter mile or more to where the shallow stream broke musically across a gravel bar. The unknown rider had crossed here and—Tavener also taking the ford—had threaded the willow strip, striking definitely toward Lily Cordray's Hat Ranch four miles northeast. A fuller darkness caught Tavener here and he trespassed forbidden soil. Facing about then, he cantered back to the road which separated Hat from Turkey Track, and rode toward Sun-

123

down, announcing itself by winking light points through the steady pour.

"One of her men cruised my range, came back to the bridge and refused to cross it," he pondered. "Why? And what brought him over there in the first place?" All the weight of his mind pressed on the fact, for at twenty-five, Matt Tavener knew the storms of the White Cloud country never broke unannounced. Stray bits of flotsam came up on the preliminary wind; the planned campaigns of men foreshadowed themselves by such surreptitious pieces of evidence as these tracks. Standing alone they meant nothing; later fragments would make the story complete. Laying the matter in a corner of his mind, Tavener lifted his slicker collar and bent gently beneath the thickening drip, thinking that here was the first tangible admission of that wholly immaterial warning he had felt for several days.

At a faster rack he covered the few miles and fell into Sundown's single street, going along the darkly graceful double row of locusts, in and out of yellow bays of lamplight lapping against the shadows. There was a crowd. Men stirred casually over the boards and music undulated out of the Masonic Hall's second story, where the Saturday dance had begun. Finding a hole for his horse, he saw most of the Turkey Track crew stationed near Syl Pennoyer's pool room, more strictly cohering than idle men should. He hadn't moved a yard before Idewall Jones, his foreman, sauntered up. Idewall's hazel eyes were watchful under his hat brim; one hand cupped a cigarette from the rain while the other made a hitching gesture.

"Big jag of Hat men around."

"The easiest way to start anything," Matt told him impatiently, "is to stand over there and look tough."

"There is something funny. I don't get it, but there sure is. Cash Vane's in tonight. His nag's in Gault's stable. I—"

His face became instantly indifferent. Dan McCarty, sheriff of White Cloud, advanced at a slow, loosefooted walk, his big body suggesting something slow to start and hard to stop. Near Tavener his head lifted and Matt saw the official's face to be smoother than usual. McCarty made a drifting sort of halt and said, "Hello, Matt," without much inflection.

"Hello, Dan."

"Funny weather for August," murmured the sheriff. He stirred, showed a touch of uncertainty; and his glance remained a little longer on Tavener, cooly speculating. Then he passed on. Idewall Jones' voice was a mere purr.

"What's eatin' him? I told you something was dam' queer."

Matt smiled. Idewall Jones was a sound man, not easily rattled. But he had the superstitions of a cat and these, playing on his hereditary antagonism toward Hat, made him spooky. "I want no trouble tonight," Matt warned him. "You hold that crew tight." Idewall said something below his breath as Matt turned in the direction of the Masonic Hall. A cluster of stags stood at the foot of the stairs, risking pneumonia in the fragrant rain; Matt acknowledged the general welcome and walked up, at once touched by the warmth of the lights and the music and the cheerful confusion.

It was a pretty picture, all the women's dresses shining and turning under the colored lanterns, but he had no intention of becoming a part of it until he saw Lily Cordray and found the girl's glance touching him. And then it was like a shock, that suggestion of appeal so fugitively crossing the room; for whatever once had been between them was only history now, and had been for a year. She was a slim, supple-bodied girl, buoyed up by a quiet pride that gave definition to all her gestures and talk; a bright and yellow-haired figure surrounded by three solemn, saddle-colored Hat stalwarts. Her eyes slipped away from Matt and she smiled at someone, the effect of it very vivid. Feeling the pull of that smile, as he always did, he thought somberly that they once might have had a chance, even with the family quarrel casting its smoky shadow across their hopes. But the possibility had quite vanished with the death of the elders; and now that each ruled his respective outfit, their feudal obligations made the thing beyond any reckoning. He thought this bitterly, assailed by a sense of heavy loss, and caught a second time that fleeting survey. It was, somehow, imperative. Slow excitement coursed through Tavener and he was inwardly irritated when a couple paused and a girl said teasingly: "When are you going to ask me, Matt?" His grin was brittle around the lip corners. Slipping by, he walked through the weaving dancers, this moment regretting the height that invariably made a target of him. When he reached Lily Cordray's side her eyes were coolly impersonal, a bit of acting, he recognized, for the benefit of those Hat men lowering at him.

He said: "Care to dance around?"

One of the riders cut in. "Tavener—"

Lily Cordray stilled that with a curt phrase. "Be quiet, Henry." Then she said formally, "How are you, Matt," and acepted his arm. They went wheeling away and Tavener, looking over the top of that tawny head, saw astonishment run through the hall at the spectacle of their being together. She moved with a lithe grace and her arms touched him with the faintest of weight.

"Anything I can do?" he asked.

"Nothing."

"Something you wanted to tell me?"

"Stay out of this, Matt."

"What?"

They were half around. Lily Cordray's chin rose, to bring her gray, even eyes against his own puzzled glance. A long and cloudy shadow lay across those eyes, dimming the gaiety that should have been there. "I'd accuse you of anything but stupidity. Stay out of this."

"That's all?"

"Yes."

Matt laid an iron silence on his tongue. They could not cross that high wall the year had built between, nor ever recapture the lost understanding. They had grown up, beyond the reckless dreams of youth. He was in the Hat corner again, feeling the gentle pushing pressure of her arms, and he stopped and stepped away. "I'm obliged," he said, instantly turning off. Idewall Jones was at the moment near the stair landing, dry face mirroring shock. Matt ignored the man and went down to the street, pausing briefly there to roll a cigarette among the stags. Then he walked on into the rain, Idewall moving doggedly abreast.

"What in hell was the reason for that?"

Matt said nothing.

"No good will ever come of parleyin' with a Cordray," said Idewall. "You're old enough to know it." And he wheeled away, angry clear through. Matt strolled as far as Gault's stable and paused inside the arch, hearing the murmured assault of rain on the high roof and the low stamp of the stalled ponies. He paced backward quickly, got beside a vague buckskin shape, and dropped; he didn't need a match. Lifting one of the buckskin's hoofs he passed a hand across it and rose, fully satisfied.

"It was Vane who came across my grass and refused to go over the bridge. Why?" The question became increasingly important. He went to the street again and headed diagonally for Syl Pennoyer's, noting that his crew had gone—into the saloon, he supposed. Idewall Jones, whose vigilance was like that of a mothering hen, sidled from the shadows and spoke with an increase of restless wonder. "McCarty wants to see you."

Matt thought, "Now we'll get the meaning of this," and continued forward. The sheriff's office door was open and the falling rain laid straight crystal filaments across the light. When he entered he found not only the sheriff there but Lily Cordray. She stood silent and calm, yet her eyes reached Tavener and plainly warned him. Idewall Jones was stopped on the threshold by McCarty's easy suggestion. "This is private."

Idewall, more and more suspicious, showed a balkiness that Matt had to check. "Go on back to the crew." Then the foreman faded and another figure stepped out of the rain and paused before them—Cash Vane. He was not very tall and not very heavy; a man plainly controlled by quick nerves. Wariness rode every motion he made and the light, slanting

127

across a darkly angular countenance, heightened the simmering arrogance on it. A cigarette clung damply to one corner of his mouth. His eyes slid across the three with a fluid speed and something happened to his cheeks. They seemed to freeze.

McCarty laid both heavy arms on the desk before him. "Gib LaTouche," he said, "was found in the rocks at Burnt Meadow this afternoon. He had been dead all night. A forty-four bullet through his chest." He announced it conversationally, as if it could be no surprise to them. None of them, at least, showed surprise. Matt Tavener thought, "This is it," and his attention returned to Lily Cordray, whose shoulders had squared at the first word. Her cheeks, ivory in their paleness, had gone queerly poker-tight, like Cash Vane's. Vane reached for a match on the sheriff's desk and lighted his smoke, negligence too pronounced. "What do you know about it?" McCarty asked the girl.

"Nothing."

"He was your foreman. When did he leave home quarters?"

"Yesterday after supper. To ride line over against the Turkey Track boundary."

"Alone?"

"Yes," she said. Matt Tavener heard a faint slowness in the answer.

"Well," said the sheriff, "he dragged his picket some. He was on Tavener ground. Why? You people ain't in the habit of visitin'."

"He wasn't stealing any Tavener beef," interjected the girl. "Gib was an honest man. I never knew a better foreman."

"Any ideas, then?" pressed the sheriff.

"No." Once more Matt got that suggestion of reluctance. It warned and disturbed him more then all the talk. McCarty swung his way.

"Did you know Gib was riding your side?"

"It's news to me."

"Maybe one of your men saw him."

Tavener thought about that. "No," he decided. "Nobody's

128

been that far west since Friday. No beef in the meadow this time of the year."

The sheriff's palms turned down on the desk. "A Hat foreman killed on Turkey Track. You know what will be thought, don't you? With plenty reason and plenty precedent."

Tavener shrugged his shoulders. "No truth in it." Then he spoke more bluntly. "The country expects us to tie into each other. That was the way of it when my dad ran Turkey Track and Bob Cordray operated Hat. Twenty years of dog fighting. Not any more. The old quarrel's burnt out and I won't start it again."

"Sounds nice," observed McCarty. "But not reasonable."

"I realize," said Matt dryly, "that the spectators want the old show to go on."

McCarty's eyes divided a steady glance between Lily Cordray and Matt. "An agreement between you two?"

"No," Matt answered. "None."

McCarty swung to Cash Vane. "What do you know?"

"Nothing," murmured Vane. His eyes went over to Tavener, pale green coloring very cold against a blackened skin. The hostility in them was a still, motionless thing.

McCarty said, abruptly: "That's all till I call you again," and appeared to lose interest. Lily Cordray walked quietly through the doorway, Cash Vane wheeling behind her. Seeing that, Matt remembered how this Vane had so invariably protected the rear of the old Bob Cordray in the other days. The habits of a gunman never changed; nor his fierce adherence to a bloody tradition. Tavener, in the rain again, watched Lily Cordray go directly to her horse. The rest of Hat was assembling. Idewall Jones drifted out of darkness. "I heard about LaTouche. They ain't goin' to pin that on you."

"Find the boys. We're going home."

"Hat can have all the trouble it wants," snapped Idewall, going off. Half a dozen men stood in front of the nearby Pennoyer's, quietly talking. One of them, Tavener was surprised to see, was a Hat man making no effort to rejoin his party. Idling that way, he heard the fellow say: "I was fired. I don't ride for Hat no more." Then he swung doubtfully on Tavener. "Hello, Matt. Need a hand?"

"Next week, maybe."

Lily Cordray was in the saddle, waiting, sitting like a soldier; and once more Matt was oddly affected. Music poured down the Masonic Hall stairway and the saloon rumble spread outward as the Turkey Track men emerged. One of the idlers near Matt said amusedly: "Well, Vane served her daddy and he'll serve her. Why don't she marry him?"

It was the way it was said. Matt Tavener whipped around, fallen into a cold, consuming rage. He slapped the fellow on the mouth twice, knocking him against the store wall. His voice sounded husky and strange in his own ears. "Watch your tongue or I'll tie something on it!"

Idewall plunged ahead, quick to anticipate trouble. Turkey Track advanced and surrounded Matt—a piece of strategy out of the older days, needing no rehearsal. All the Hat people were mounted and motionless, making a black line against the buildings. There was danger here, for Cash Vane had turned and he was waiting as only a man who desires to have a fight waits. The embittered, unreasoning hatred of these crews was a substantial presence on the street. That tautness lasted but a moment. Lily Cordray's level voice broke it. "Come on." Cash Vane didn't immediately obey but the rest of Hat moved out after her and soon faded beyond town. Watching Cash, Matt saw the man look around in astonishment at this desertion. A moment later he followed.

"Is that what's put the shadow on her face?" wondered Matt. "Tryin' to ho!d him back?"

"Ain't we wet enough without standin' here?" muttered Idewall Jones.

Somebody touched Matt Tavener's arm and he turned to find Judge Lummis standing beneath an ancient umbrella. The judge's face was old and brought to a point by a Vandyke turned white; and he spoke with the liberty of a friendship to the family that went back before Matt's own twenty-five years. "Are you makin' overtures to that girl?"

"Tell me you don't like it," said Matt grimly.

"If she meant to play fair with you, why has she got Cash Vane on the place, who was her father's paid killer?"

"The trouble with this country," rapped out Matt, "is that it won't mind its own business. The spectators figure the show too tame."

"If she meant——"

Tavener swung speechless to his horse and went whirling out of Sundown with Turkey Track behind. A little wind had risen and the rain drove freshly against his face; the night was black, without a star. His thoughts, very clear and very bitter, ran like quicksilver. Three generations of White Cloud people had been born into the Cordray-Tavener fight. It was fixed history, a part of their lives; and now they would not forgive him for letting it die. The weight of that opinion balked him and even the Turkey Track hands, loyal as they were, had the madness of the violent past in their blood. White Cloud considered the quarrel a piece of public property he had no right to touch. Idewall, directly behind was muttering.

"Vane's a man that was born to kill. Like a cougar. Bob Cordray hired him for that—and he did his job well. He's spent his life learnin' all the tricks of blastin' holes in poor devils that never had time to get the same skill. Nobody can touch him. Only way is to surround him and let him have it. This LaTouche business stinks."

The Sixes River bridge lay darkly ahead. Judge Lummis' words came back. "Why does she keep Cash Vane?" He pressed down on the reins and Turkey Track overran him and circled curiously back. Idewall Jones queried. "What's up?" But Matt was thinking he had stayed away from Lily Cordray too long. If she needed help she wouldn't ask for it. "What's up?" repeated Idewall.

"Go on home," ordered Matt and cut down the north side of Sixes River, alone.

In Sundown, Judge Lummis pointed his unforgiving, matter-of-fact face at the sheriff. "Let it ride, McCarty. Go no farther."

131

"It's murder."

"It used to be called retribution. I don't doubt a Turkey Track man got LaTouche. LaTouche was old enough to know he had no business on the wrong side of the road. He got what many a Tavener hand got for trespassin'. Let it ride."

McCarty seemed to be trying to remember something. "There used to be something between those two young people, Judge."

"Maybe once, but not now. How can they rule those outfits and like each other? Not in a thousand years. I drew up every legal paper Len Tavener had to make. I watched him grow and I watched him turn gray fightin' Bob Cordray. No mercy given, none asked. There's no good in softness now and if Matt don't know that I'll tell him."

"There's something," mused the sheriff, racking his memory, "that just slips out from under my finger. LaTouche was a peaceful man. Why should he be killed?"

Lily Cordray went into the Hat house, closed the door and walked to the heat of the fireplace, stripping off her slicker. She had her back to the door, but when it opened she knew who had entered; and for a moment she stood rigidly still. The monotony of Cash Vane's voice was like the deceiving monotony of his face.

"So LaTouche," he said, "went over on the Turkey Track side to prob'ly follow strays. And Tavener got him."

Not looking at him, she said: "Where were you yesterday?"

"Ridin' the east line." His voice turned metallic. "It's your fault, Lily. You've been runnin' a pussyfoot show since your dad died. You made Gib foreman because he was soft and would mind you. It didn't work. It never will work. Hat is a fightin' outfit. That crew in the bunkhouse rode under old Bob in better days and they're willing to ride again, under me. We'll take care of this killin'."

She had known from the beginning he despised the peace she kept. Once having been her father's gunman, he could

132

not tolerate a loss of power. The man was sleepless in his desire for vengeance, full of scheming desires. What she had feared ever since taking charge was about to come fatally true. The sense of it entered the room with him.

"Get this, Cash. You'll give no orders to the crew. I'm running Hat."

"Running it into the ground. Old Bob would turn in his grave."

"You'll mind me or you'll go."

"You've tried to get rid of me before," he told her, arrogantly obstinate. "It didn't work. There ain't a man on the place that will back you up in that. I ran Hat for old Bob and I'll run it for you. Tonight I fired Ken Weed, which you made a mistake hirin'. He was soft, like LaTouche."

In the motionless depth of his eyes she could see the jealous temper there—a temper even her own father had occasionally sidestepped. "Listen to me," she argued, "we've had this out before. You're living in the past."

"You're trying to protect Matt Tavener," accused Vane. "I always knew that. You don't want him hurt. It was a pretty play he made tonight. I heard why. He belted that man down because the fellow said something about you. It won't work, Lily. If you've got no pride about Hat, we have."

Lily Cordray's mobile face was modeled in stubbornness. "I warn you, Cash."

He laughed then, a short and violent laugh. "Was you a man I could lick some sense into you, which old Bob would have wanted."

The anger in her chilled to desperation. Her hands made an odd gesture. "All right! If you go over my head I'll use a gun on you! I mean that!"

"By God—!"

The door opened, letting in a gush of wind that momentarily sucked away the light of the lamps. Matt Tavener swung through, closed the door and leaned against it; between hat brim and slicker collar his face was shaded, sharply observant, and pointed at Vane. Vane stood still.

"Get out," ordered Tavener. "I want to talk with Lily."

133

"No," contradicted the girl. "Stay here, Cash."

But Vane had made his own decision before then, and he went swiftly to the door, opened it and slammed it behind. Lily Cordray said, desperately: "He'll have the crew on top of you."

"Lily, what can I do to help you?"

She supported herself against the corner of the fireplace, body going lax. "I told you to keep out of this, Matt," she told him, sounding dead tired.

"I have kept out of it for a year."

"That isn't enough."

"Why?"

"Don't ask that!"

"So a Tavener can have nothing to do with a Cordray? You thought different once. Who changed the rules for you?"

"Never mind."

"You're in trouble, Lily. I had nothing to do with Gib LaTouche. I liked him. He was the only man you had who would keep the peace for you."

"You don't need to tell me. And Matt—I'd never fight you. Never."

"Then, why do we let this fool game go on?" he broke out.

She didn't answer and he felt himself against a barrier he couldn't cross. So he said gently, "That's all, Lily?"

"Good luck."

Tavener's shoulders rose a little and he made a slow turn for the door. Lily called out, "Wait," and went in front of him. It was obvious protection, but he saw nobody in the dark yard just then. When he got to the saddle he saw her face was dim and strained and wistful. "Everybody," he said, "wants the old show to go on except you and me. There's a limit to family pride, Lily."

"Don't come back. If we want peace we've got to buy it— by staying apart." Then her voice went flat. "Goodby."

He trotted across the yard. On its edge he turned and found Cash Vane's thin and familiar silhouette in the bunk-house doorway. He knew, he knew beyond any doubt then.

134

All the stray facts joined to make the story complete. Vane had killed LaTouche to usurp the power of Hat. Realizing it, he raced into the valley.

What drew him into town the following afternoon was a message from the sheriff. A considerable wind drove ragged clouds across the western peaks, broke them and spilled rain along a forty-mile strip. In Sundown at that hour lights were burning and all the building doors, normally open from May till October, were closed against the slanting, crystal fusillade. When he entered McCarty's office he knew what to expect, having seen the two Hat ponies racked outside. Lily Cordray stood where she had been the previous night, the same subdued tautness holding her. Cash Vane faced the door, cat-like in his regard of them all.

McCarty said: "Of course it's murder. What time did you start from Turkey Track yesterday?"

"About six-thirty."

"Notice any hoof marks along the road, or crossing the road?"

Matt wondered how McCarty would be guessing that. But he shook his head and said, "No." The sheriff couldn't expect anything of him but a lie. Such answer as was to be made would come out in the hills where all this had begun; and the affair lay between himself and Cash Vane. Along the intervening hours he had worked out his own part, which was the part White Cloud understood best—a challenge and a shot.

"Where were you, Cash?" demanded McCarty.

"Riding the eastern Hat fence."

"That right, Lily?"

"Yes."

"Anybody have a quarrel on Hat with Gib?"

Matt didn't look at her. Her soft, "Not to my knowledge," was the reply he knew she would make. It was part of the game. What interested him then was the straining, threatening fire in Cash Vane's eyes as they clung to the girl. McCarty drummed the table with his knuckles.

"This business goes logically back to Turkey Track. Gib

135

was riding on the wrong side of the road. You people starting another war?"

"If you want your answer to Gib LaTouche," said Tavener slowly, "go up where you found him and look again."

"After two days' rain? It's washed out."

"Never mind. Go look again."

McCarty's face tipped up, suddenly shrewd. The silence went thin. Lily Cordray's body swayed gently and that deep glow began to strengthen through the shadows along her brow. Matt never looked at Vane; the man seemed to have diminished into the farthest edge of his vision. McCarty sighed a little. "That's all. I'm going to get to the bottom of this."

Lily Cordray turned with a surprising swiftness, shoulder brushing Matt as she passed, so near that he saw the pulse beating at the base of her neck. On the porch, he watched her mount and go spurring into the gloomy day. Vane came out, more leisurely in his movements, looking straight ahead. He didn't follow the girl, Matt noticed, but cut back of Sundown, bound in some other direction. Reaching his own pony, Matt thought: "The oldest trap in the world, but it may work." Thereafter he went posting into the valley. Lily Cordray was ahead a matter of two miles, when the crease of the river hid her from sight. Of Vane nothing was to be seen.

"It may work," repeated Tavener and crossed the bridge at a faster gait. Beyond the bridge a little distance, he turned into a coulee climbing to the low spine of the western ridge. This he followed into a belt of pines. Thus sheltered, he wheeled across the higher, rougher ground while the day turned grayer and the rain came down in collected ropes. Dead needles swirled before the wind. One dim dome advanced out of the sleazy atmosphere and when Tavener circled this the pines fell behind and he halted at the margin of a small meadow strewn with slab rock.

Relief overtook him. This was the end of his seeking, as he had hoped. Out there in the center of the area, Cash Vane's pony stood wheeling about the dropped reins and

136

Cash Vane's lithe body ducked up and down the broken terrain with a hasting agility, seeking that evidence Matt Tavener had hinted might be carelessly left behind.

"The fool believed me," thought Tavener. "The oldest—"

One long-reaching echo came banging across the meadow, a sound fractured by the rising wind. Cash Vane sprang behind a rock and stared all about, torso crouched like that of some animal brought to stand; and Matt Tavener, deeply astonished at this interruption, lifted his glance to the meadow's farther edge and discovered Lily Cordray placed there, rifle half raised. But he had only a moment to see her, for Vane had located him and Vane was coming on with the quickness of a terrier.

That too astonished him. Poised under the rain, slicker ripped back, he made a solid shape against such light as there was—wondering at the deep, changeless hatred which could make a human fling himself so greedily at the business of destruction. The rifle spoke no more. Vane reached a rock a hundred yards off and scaled it. He jumped down, landing on all fours and savagely springing up. Never stirring, Matt Tavener eyed the narrowing distance with the remote thought that Vane's life had been a thing of savage survival, that he never had been touched, never had been slow. It was that single-minded confidence and that will to fight which drove him on now. Then Vane was in front of him, near enough for him to catch one fair view of the drawn and hungry lines on the man's features. Vane cried something that raced by Tavener on the wind; and Tavener, feeling neither emotion nor nerves, drew and sent a shot against the sudden-halted body. The echo flooded back into his face, accompanied by Cash Vane's high, sardonic yell. In the same gathered calm Tavener laid his barrel more surely on the target and let the hammer fall as an answering bullet lifted the spitting dirt at his feet. What he heard then was a faint, fading cry somehow reminding him of a wild bird traveling south in the high sky. Afterward, Vane's arms rose gauntly above, and with that gesture he faded against the drab earth, the ill light merging him with rock and soil.

Tavener let a long, slow breath out of him. "This is what she tried to avoid for the last year," he muttered. "But he's dead and his reputation helped him none." Lily Cordray galloped headlong across the meadow, her hat gone, her rifle dropped. She wrenched the horse to a stop and half fell beside him, and when he caught her he felt the shuddering of her body. All the tawny hair lay wetly to her temples. He thought she was crying, though he couldn't be sure because of the steady rain beating down her cheeks. One thing alone was certain—the scar of fear grew dimmer and dimmer in her eyes, giving way to that old, vital warmth he once had known.

"I tried to warn you with that shot, Matt! I knew you were laying a trap and I thought he had guessed it and was waiting for you to come! I didn't think you could beat him—not Cash Vane! I would have killed him!"

He said, wanting to make it very clear: "He was the reason for this year of misery?"

She watched him, she seemed to debate. "I couldn't get rid of him, Matt. I could only do one thing, which was stay away from you, to keep him still. Even that failed today."

"Lily, was it worth the trouble?"

Her answer was half a cry. "What would it be like for me, if you were dead? You spoke of pride last night. I have no pride—not the kind that could hurt you!"

"Listen. If there's ever going to be an end, it'll have to be now. Never let White Cloud build another fence between us."

"What have I told you? What else should I say?"

He drew her on and he put his hat on her wet head. That deepened the shadows on her cheeks, but even so he saw the rising gaiety, the returning sweetness of a smile.

McCarty, coming into the meadow, thought at first his eyes were betraying him after fifty years of service. There had been two distinct figures in long yellow slickers standing apart. When next he looked there was but one. He dashed his wet sleeve across his face and looked again, to find his mistake. Those two had come together. And at that point memory supplied him with the long-sought fact. "Certainly," he said. "What I was tryin' to recall is something this dam' country quite forgot. People in love never do the things other people expect 'em to do. That's what made this business very odd till now."

GENTLEMEN STAND TOGETHER

This was the prairie country's softest twilight, with the lights of Two Dance silvering the deep dust of the street. Old John was dressing down the walk in front of Menefee's stable with the water bucket as Mark Stanhope passed by, and the smell of water and dust was very keen in the still air. Old John said, "Hello, Doc," but felt no resentment when Stanhope didn't answer. Stanhope had been here a little better than a year, and his sultry, remote preoccupations were becoming understood.

Stanhope went on to the foot of the main street and put himself at the corner of Two Dance's yellow little depot, hearing the hoarse halloo of the train rush forward, seeing its headlight wash a long beam through a gathering dark. The ragged peaks of the Wolf Mountains showed their teeth blackly against the pale shadows of the west, and the thinness of this high Wyoming air was more pronounced than it had been. A horse standing nearby stirred a little and Stanhope, who had learned cattleland's habit of identifying people by their mounts, had a good look at it. Afterward he turned his eyes to the farther side of the platform then and noticed Elsa Knightwood standing quietly there.

The train ran forward at an undiminshed speed and the roar and clash and click of it filled his body with a keen, painful nostalgia. He saw passengers' blurred faces peer through the car windows; he caught blended odors of steam

140

and smoke and cinders. The last coach slipped by and he made out the shapes of an idle party clustered on the observation platform. The suction blew up a quick dust and a paper sailed along the track and settled and presently the red and green lights of this train rushing from San Francisco to Chicago became a mere wink far down the prairie. For a moment his memories were all fresh and clear, but they dimmed as the train vanished in the distance, leaving him as he had been before, profoundly alone.

The girl came along the platform and saw him then, and stopped; and her face lifted and even in the shadows he had a view of its slim, pale pride overcast by some emotion he couldn't make out. Her body was straight, her shoulders round and well-formed. He had noticed her infrequently on the street, and had never spoken to her; but it was his sudden conviction now that she was an exile from the East like himself. She had a carriage and a manner, and these things betrayed her. She had come here, as he had come, to catch this fleeting sight of a lost world. For a moment he thought she meant to speak; instead, she turned to her horse and rode along the tracks, bound back for her small homestead west of town.

He went slowly up to Faro Charley's, into the noise of the saloon's forming crowd. When he reached the bar his own bottle and glass waited there for him, and he had one quick drink and stood awhile with his body slack, waiting for the liquor's warmth to loosen him up. A man, he morosely considered, made his own hell and kept the fires of punishment alive by refusing to forget. He should never have gone down to watch the train; it didn't help to remember what his life had once been. He filled the glass again and emptied it. He saw himself in the bright flash of the back bar's mirror, a broad and burly shape—and dropped his eyes, not caring to see more. He was still young, but there was a settled bitterness about the corners of his long lips that was not young.

A rider came out of the night and crossed the floor hurriedly. He said: "Doc, we just brought in Henry LaTouche. We took him to your place."

This man's name, Stanhope recalled, was Tony Ward, a rider from the Yellow Hill country. Crossing the street with Ward, he saw two lathered horses standing by the stable. "Accident?"

"Accident," said Ward, angrily and briefly.

A dripped thread of blood pulled them up a stairway into Stanhope's second-story office. Two men stood over a third, who lay on a leather couch with a face the color of cold ashes. The sound of that one's breathing was a clear warning to Stanhope. He laid his fingers to the man's wrist and said instantly: "Put him on the table." He took off his coat; he rolled up his sleeves and went to the cabinet beside the table. But he paused a moment to lift his hands to the light and watch them critically. Afterward he cut the man's coat and shirt deftly away with a pair of scissors. The bullet, a soft .44 slug, had struck a high rib, plowed its way upward through tissue and rested now apparently against the shoulder bones.

He reached for his chloroform and sprinkled it on a folded towel, his face severe with interest. This man was hard to kill, or else he would have been dead now; but the raggedness of that pulse bothered him. He said: "How do you feel?"

"Not much," murmured LaTouche.

Stanhope greased LaTouche's lips and nostrils, made a cone of the towel and lowered it. The other three were watching him, and Tony Ward had something to say. "You've had a lot to drink, Doc."

"Better if I had more, Tony."

There was release from thinking here, the probe between his fingers and his mind as clear as it would ever be. When he used his hands he could forget. He rolled back Henry LaTouche's eyelids and let them go. He had begun to sweat, a fine moisture sparkling against the edges of his black, unruly hair. His mouth was a tight line across the stubborn arrangement of his face. When he saw that LaTouche was ready, his head dropped and his fingers began to move in the familiar pattern of his trade. He heard the men around him breathe more heavily; and he felt proud of himself, as though something in him was still competent, still untouched by the wreck of his personal life. His questing probe touched the embedded leaden slug.

But it stopped there, for Henry LaTouche's features had changed imperceptibly and there was a feeling suddenly in the room. He laid his instrument down and had another look at the man's eyes; his fingers went against the jugular and pressed against it. He stepped back, his hands making a small gesture. "Your friend," he said emotionlessly, "is dead."

He had no idea men's eyes could show such white fury, or that death could mean so much to them. As for himself, he had neither fear of it nor respect for it. A man had to have hope to fear death; he had to love life to fear it—and he had no hope in him, no love. But the silence grew enormous, the violence of the thoughts of those three cowhands growing more oppressive.

Tony Ward grunted: "You damned drunk remittance bum!"

It didn't touch him—that hatred, that scorn. His indifference was a protective tissue, and it was that indifference which so outraged them. He went back to his basin and washed his hands. His voice was completely impersonal. "Men die."

Tony Ward said, inexpressibly outraged: "If they'd been even a horse doctor in town, we'd never brought him here! It's in my mind to take a shot at you!"

Mark Stanhope rolled down his sleeves; he put on his coat. His arms were unaccountably heavy, his head dull and stupid. "That," he said, "is less of a threat than you'd figure," and passed out of the office. Going down the stairs his knees turned weak on him and sudden shadow filled his mind. He reviewed what he had done and knew that he could have done no better; yet a crack of doubt opened, and turned him cold. He had only this one thing left, this pride of his skill. If they took that from him he would have reached the bottom.

He was in Faro Charley's place again, trying to drink up his incredible weariness. All the glitter of the place pressed against his eyeballs and the sound of men's voices was an insistent murmur. The barkeeper's face was indistinct and his voice was indistinct. "There ain't any more in that bottle, Doc."

He said, with a quick, unexplainable fury, "Did I ask you if there was?" and turned out of the place. He struck a man, and the man laughed and reached up to support him; but he had a strength in that burly, restless body that suddenly became alive. He caught hold of the man, scarcely seeing him, and threw him half across the room.

Afterward he felt the fresh thin air on his face and found he was in his own saddle, on his own horse. Looking around, he made out the lights of Two Dance far down the prairie. Directly ahead of him the foothills of the Two Dance range began to break through the night. His horse had stopped, though he couldn't understand why. A woman's voice came out across the shadows, near and clear.

"You can't go through a barb-wire fence."

He turned. There was a shanty's dark outline behind him, with a lamp's yellow flood brightly outlining the square doorway in which she stood. He had never been here before, but he knew now it was Elsa Knightwood's place. He put his horse about and rode over. The light touched him mercilessly as he sat hatless and slack in the saddle, his black hair without order on his head, a gray and bottomless expression on his stubborn face. He said, with a drunken man's care to be exact:

"I do not know how I got here."

He put his hands to the saddle horn. Everything was vague, yet the impression she made on him was distinct, the silhouette of her round strong shoulders acutely real to him. He saw her sway gently; her voice had a calmness that reached into his mind.

"Get down and come in."

"Not a wise thing."

"Do you know what wisdom is, Doctor Stanhope?"

He got down and she turned from the doorway to let him pass through. He saw a rocking chair and dropped into

144

it and put one of his big hands across his eyes. It helped a little, for when he uncovered them again he saw her more clearly. She stood against a wall and she was watching him with eyes that seemed to be hazel, that seemed to be proud—and to be sad. Her hair was a deep yellow that caught up the room's light and turned it to a rich glow. Her lips, he thought, were as a man would want them, generous and steady. She was a fair woman.

He said: "If you hope to have any peace of mind, don't watch those trains."

Her answer was softly whispered. "Is there no hope in you at all?"

He sat forward and put his elbows on his knees and ran a hand through his ruffled hair. He heard her move away, but he was too indifferent to look up. It was a mistake to suppose that drink helped a man to forget. It filled a man's head with a light that was sharp and sunless and cruel. There was a perfect clarity. The world he saw then was like the barren surface of a dead planet.

She said: "Drink this." She was in front of him, holding out a cup of coffee. He took it and hot as it was he drank it down with scarcely a breath. He balanced the cup in his hand and extended his arm full length. There was no tremor.

"Do you buy hope in sacks or barrels? It's an illusion we start life with. If we're lucky we don't lose too much of it. Otherwise we lose it all and there's never any more to be had for the buying."

She said in a wondering, wistful way: "Who could have hurt you so much?"

"Did I say anyone had?"

"Why else should you be watching that train go through?"

"A mistake we both make."

"Yes," she murmured, "I think so."

"You see," he said. "We are foolish—trying to warm our hands over a dead fire."

"You're bitter," she told him. "All the things I've heard about you, then, are true. Nothing matters to you. You aren't kind, you have no sympathy."

"Once is enough to have your heart broken. Haven't you found that out yet?" He couldn't, at the moment, get on his feet. There wasn't any strength in them. He leaned back in the rocker, hearing a man speak on the porch.

"Elsa—everything all right?"

The man coming through the door was very tall, very slim. He removed his hat with the bred politeness of his kind, to expose a head of hair as red as the sun. His was the tanned and smooth and enigmatic face of the range rider; it swung toward Mark Stanhope and wasn't pleased. Bill Tower, Stanhope understood, didn't like stray men going into Elsa Knightwood's shanty after dark. Alone as she was out here, she had this protection. Then he had a clear sight of Bill Tower's mind; for the high-built and indolent-speaking rider turned his eyes to the girl and his voice was almost humble. "You're all right?" he repeated. "I was just ridin' by."

"You know Doctor Stanhope?" said Elsa.

"Yeah," agreed Bill Tower briefly. He looked at Stanhope once more. He said: "I'll ride a ways with you, Doc."

Stanhope pushed himself to his feet. The coffee had cleared his head a little. "The morals of the situation, Bill," he observed ironically, "are all on your side." This room was neat and small; and there was a picture on the wall that caught his fancy. It was a drawing cut from a magazine, of some New England meadow deep in snow. The sight and smell of that far-away country was in the drawing, the sense of it very keen in this prairie room.

"Another memory you do wrong to keep," he observed. "You've traveled two thousand miles to forget it, haven't you?"

She was watching him, she was listening to the downbearing, indifferent tones of his voice; and the fairness of her face seemed to catch the darkness of his feeling. Her shoulders rested against the wall; they dropped a little. "Have you no hope in you at all?" she murmured.

"Whisky is better."

She was at once angry. Color turned her cheeks beautiful and brought back the vigor of her slender, supple body. She still had a resistance to the dismal brutalities of the world; and the recognition of that brought up in him a feeling that was half pleased and half sad. She would keep on fighting— and be hurt the more. She said: "At least you could have courage."

"But for what?" he asked. Bill Tower was a grave, attentive shape in the background. He was listening to this, and not comprehending it; he was outside this talk—an alien to the world that had produced Elsa Knightwood and Mark Stanhope. Some remote instinct of courtesy caused Mark Stanhope to apologize. "We shouldn't be speaking in a foreign language when you're here, Bill." And he bowed at Elsa Knightwood solemnly and went out to his horse. He had a little trouble getting into the saddle and he heard Elsa Knightwood speak very softly to Tower. "Please look after him." Riding back along the prairie, toward Two Dance's distant lights, he found Tower beside him.

The air had a thin, cool freshness; the moonlight laid its silver frost particles along the shadowed earth. The edge of his liquor was gone and depression pushed him farther and farther into the blank bottom regions of his being. He considered his professional judgment with a straining patience and found nothing wrong; he had had to take that chance with Henry LaTouche. The man's ticket simply ran out. Yet Tony Ward's eyes, so charged with rage and disbelief, were vivid in his memory. If they destroyed the pride he had in his skill he'd have nothing left at all.

He came into Two Dance and left his horse and wearily climbed the stairs to his office, Bill Tower creaking along behind. They had removed LaTouche's body. Stanhope stood by the table a moment, gripped by his thoughts. Bill Tower leaned against the wall, shaping up a cigarette. Tower said: "A woman livin' alone on the prairie stands some risk. Drunks have no business ridin' over there. Damn you, stay away from her!"

Stanhope turned, remotely curious. Bill Tower's eyes were smoky, they showed the raggedness of his feelings.

"You're a gentleman, Bill. And you're right."

Bill Tower stared at Stanhope, at once past anger. He had anxiety on his smooth cheeks, he had the print of a long puzzle there. "What's hurt that girl, Doc?"

"Why ask me?"

"You two," murmured Bill Tower, "are alike. You're both from the East. You ought to know. If it was a man and I knew where he was I'd go bust his neck." He spun violently around on his heels and left the room.

Stanhope supported himself momentarily by the table. His nerves were bad; they were snapping and snarling inside him. He said, "I've got to have a drink," and rounded toward the door. But he set his will against that rising appetite and went into his adjoining bedroom. He took off his coat and his shoes, and rolled under the blankets. A man got pretty low when he forgot to take off his clothes; but he was too tired to care.

Beyond breakfast time, the flashing heat of summer already laying its pressure on the baked boards of the town, he strolled up the shady side of the street and saw Bill Tower waiting for him by the corner of Walt Driscoll's stable. Bill Tower tossed away a cigarette; he fell into step beside Stanhope and they went along a full fifty feet. Tower's tall body swayed indolently as he stepped across the boards. His eyelids were half closed, setting up fine wrinkles at the corners. He said then, as casual as springtime's wind:

"Tony Ward has made some remarks about you. He took Henry LaTouche's dyin' right serious. The two were strong friends. You know Tony's reputation?"

"A crook."

"Inclined to be quick on the move," remarked Bill Tower.

Mark Stanhope shook his head, having nothing then to say. Their walking had taken them past the deep porch of the hotel; and beyond was a straggling road leading westward across the tawny prairie. Stanhope turned that way.

"It is plain," murmured Bill Tower, "the man means to meet you."

They were then standing in back of the town. Stanhope

stopped. "Let me have your gun, Bill."

Bill Tower came about; he put his hands on his hips, staring down with a bright curiosity. This black-headed, burly man was a puzzle to him, plainly. But he obeyed, handing over his .44. Stanhope weighed the gun in his right hand, balancing it in his palm. He raised it and saw along its sights the upright shape of an old post thirty yards away. He fired at it five times, and lowered the gun.

Bill Tower swung. He paced the distance to the post, and looked carefully at the splintered results of Stanhope's shooting; and paced back. He said, quietly: "Where'd you learn to do that?"

"Tell Tony Ward you saw it done," suggested Stanhope. "It may change his mind."

"You've made it worse than it was." Half a dozen townsmen sauntered forward to discover what this meant, and Tower watched them irritably. "The town might not've stood for Tony pullin' a gun on a man unhandy with weapons. But you've made it an equal contest—and now you've got a fight for sure."

"Wait," said Stanhope. "Why do you care?"

Bill Tower's shoulders rose, and they fell. He bowed his head over his fingers, tapering up a cigarette. He was dissatisfied, he was taciturn. "It was somethin' you said," he answered reluctantly, and then went away.

"You do that, Doc?" said one of the townsmen.

Mark Stanhope returned to Two Dance's main street. The smell of dust was in the air, and the scorched odor of the building walls became more pronounced. Life in this town began to dry up and flow sluggishly. He went up to his office and washed his hands; and thrust them in front of him, watching his steady fingertips with a critical, dark attention. What had he failed to do in the case of Henry LaTouche that he might have done? He drew a long breath and picked up his doctor's satchel and went down the stairs.

He had his chores to do, and was grateful to have them so that the morning might pass without too much thought. When he was finished he came back up the street and ran into Faro Charley. "I hear," Faro Charley said, "you can use a gun. Carry one?"

"No."

Faro Charley moved his cigar from the left to the right side of his mouth. "Better if you djd," he murmured, and went away. Up in his office, Stanhope found the heat greater than usual. He put his instruments back into the cabinet and sat by the table, with his elbows on it, and quietly sweated. In this country he was still a tenderfoot, and thus protected against the roughness of the range temper. But he had proved to Two Dance that he could handle a gun and now Two Dance, obeying its strict conscience in the matter, would let him handle his own quarrels.

He thought of that indifferently. It was noon then, with his nerves crawling again. He needed a drink; yet he had set his first-drink deadline at three o'clock and there was a bitter stubbornness in him against that appetite which kept growing stronger and stronger. He had a sudden fear he could not keep his resolve; and abruptly he left his office and went to the stable for his horse. He rode to the south, to Elsa Knightwood's small house.

It was a pleasant spot beside the low banks of a little creek flowing down from the footslopes of the nearby Two Dance range; a group of cottonwoods shaded the house and there was a garden along the creek, with corn standing high in it, and a home-made irrigation ditch running through it. Bill Tower's horse stood in the yard. When Stanhope rounded the house he found the cowhand idly crouched on the steps, and Elsa Knightwood seated in a porch chair. Stanhope recognized the remote displeasure in Tower's eyes, but the power of the girl's presence drew his attention to her instantly. There was a pleasantness and a sense of peace there, and her supple figure, even in the chair, stirred in him the memory of a fire strongly burning. He got down and came over to the porch, conscious that Tower had risen and stepped a little backward, as though to be out of the way.

"I owe you an apology for last night."

She rose with a quickness that was strange to him, and her

smile was strong and sweet and womanly. She had a pride that gave to her words a slow and stirring melody; that made the hot day unimportant, that touched him in the way high wind might touch him. "Don't."

He said, quietly: "It isn't that I spoke anything less than what I believe to be the truth. But I had no real right to speak it to you."

Her smile faded with his talk; and a darkness deepened and became intense in her eyes. She said: "Oh," in a falling, disappointed tone.

He looked out upon the garden. He said: "You've done all this yourself?"

"You have your way of forgetting, and I have my way."

"Has your way helped you?"

"Self pity isn't a pretty thing. Perhaps you think it very dramatic when you get drunk and make Two Dance believe you're ruining yourself in a handsome, reckless fashion. I don't think so. I think you've lost your courage."

"Why do you care?"

"I don't," she said. "I don't in the least."

He bowed quietly and turned. Young Bill Tower hadn't moved. He stood very still, effacing himself from this scene out of courtesy. It was the way he looked at the girl, Stanhope considered, that betrayed him. The man loved her. In his own faithful manner he was gallant—he was a gentleman. Stanhope got on his horse and circled back toward Two Dance. It was one o'clock, two hours away from the time set for the first drink. All his nerves were like hot, short-circuited wires in him and he knew if he reached Two Dance he would break his rule. He pointed his horse northward, resolving not to go into town until three o'clock came.

The girl watched him go, her glance full of shadow. Bill Tower saw that long, sad look. He lowered his head, slowly creasing the crown of his hat between his fingers. He said: "How long have you known him?"

Her words were gentle with him. "It isn't a matter of time, Bill. He's my sort. I know him thoroughly—so thoroughly. Help him if you can."

Bill Tower said, "Yeah," and watched the expression on her face with a patient interest.

At three o'clock, Mark Stanhope walked into Faro Charley's saloon and took his drink. He put his elbows on the bar and rested his weight there, his black head attentively bowed. Whisky, to him, was like the oil that ships cast overboard in times of distress to break the force of the high seas. He waited there for that drink to smooth the bitter turbulence that kept reaching higher and higher during his sober hours. Hope was a thing that made life rich; a bottle and a glass were for those who had no hope. He filled his glass a second time and saw Faro Charley looking across the bar at him with the careful glance of a man who means not to interfere.

"I heard it said," remarked Faro Charley, "that Tony Ward was to be in town at supper time."

Mark Stanhope moved his heavy shoulders and went out of the saloon, walking in a straight, swinging, impatient manner. In his office he stood a moment beside the table, thinking once again, with an unrelenting preciseness, of what he had done for Henry LaTouche. The heat of the room was very heavy and sweat started down his forehead and made all his body humid. He shucked off his coat and lay down on the cot nearby. The clanking sound of the Yellow Hill stage came through the open window. It was the heat that turned his thinking backward to a gentle lane through Boston's elms, to the softness and pleasantness of life there, to the shape and color of things so old, so familiar, so well-remembered. His will, his pure will, closed the curtain on that with a bitter compulsion.

Long afterward the supper bell from the restaurant brought him up from the cot. It was six o'clock then—the time Tony Ward meant to be in Two Dance. Considering this, he felt a remote surprise at knowing that he had come to accept the ethics of cattle land in the matter. He had to be down there to meet Ward, for he had put five shots into a post at thirty paces and was a pilgrim no longer.

He went down the stairs. The sun was behind the western range, its hot rays like artillery blasts in the high sky; but along the walks the quick violet twilight already was settling, softening the town's angular unloveliness. He stopped a moment, as if to register his presence, and then identified Bill Tower idle against a porch post higher up the street. Bill Tower made no motion at him, and Stanhope went into the hotel and ate his supper; and came out into a bluer dusk flowing like water through Two Dance's alleys. The false fronts of the buildings cut sharp, black silhouettes against the sky's night blue. A man behind him said, calmly:

"I hear you can shoot."

He knew who that would be before he turned; and came about slowly, to find Tony Ward there, against the hotel wall. Ward said, "Do you carry a gun?" But he was scanning Mark Stanhope with a keen glance and had his own answer. He added, "Go get one," and swung on his heels, marching up the street. Looking that way, Stanhope saw Bill Tower still rooted to his long-held position.

There was one spot in Stanhope's mind that kept wondering and marveling at his own actions as he went stolidly back up the office stairs. This was a ritual he had seen other men of the country observe strictly. Now he was going through the ritual, not knowing why. In his room he found his revolver, long unused, and opened its cylinder to observe the loads there. He held the gun a moment in his hand, weighing it. He had, he observed, no perceptible fear, and afterward started down the stairs.

Not quite at the bottom, he heard a play of gunshots roll in hard, detonating waves along the street. It sent him down the last steps in one wide jump, for he had quick comprehension of what it was, of what it meant. Men were rushing up from Faro Charley's and out of the hotel. He was in the rear of this forming crowd as it swung by the livery stable and passed on into the adjoining alley. But he jammed his shoulders against these people and knocked them aside—and came upon Bill Tower lying on the cluttered dust, slightly risen on one elbow. Vague as the light was, he saw the quick paling of Tower's face. He dropped on one knee, and put an arm around Tower, hearing a man farther along the alley say, "Tony's altogether dead." But his own voice was angry and strange to him.

"Where are you hit?"

Somebody came forward with a lantern. Mark Stanhope got his hands around Bill Tower. He lifted that long body with no great effort. He threw his talk at the crowd. "Get the hell out of here!" and he went across the street and up the stairs. Faro Charley was directly behind, and one other man, and they came into the office and stood silent while Stanhope laid Tower on the table. The bullet, he saw, had struck somewhere around the left pelvic bone, with a good deal of fresh blood coming out; and there was a gray, gaunt look around Tower's mouth. But his eyes were open and his pulse was strong.

"Why?" grunted Stanhope.

Bill Tower smiled faintly. "Well, you said I was a gentleman. I never been dealt that hand before. Be damned if I knew how to play it—but I did what seemed right."

Mark Stanhope cut away Bill Tower's trousers and looked down at the bullet's battered entry. His mouth changed a little. He got out a towel and folded it and sprinkled it with chloroform. Bill Tower's eyes grew shrewder.

"Take off my boots."

It was Faro Charley who first understood the urgency of that request and came forward to obey. Stanhope laid a damp cloth over Tower's eyes to protect them, and greased the man's lips and nose against the bite of the anesthetic; and then applied the cone-shaped chloroform towel. Laying out his instruments beside him, he put his hands on the edge of the table and gripped it with all the force of his fingers; and suddenly a complete darkness whirled through him. Faro Charley said, "Now, Doc."

The darkness went away. He touched Bill Tower's pulse and looked into Tower's eyes. He picked up his probe, and held it poised in his fingers, and saw that it had no tremor. His black head dropped toward his task; he was cool and sure of himself, and his fingers followed a routine, without flaw.

When he was finished—when he was quite finished—and had laid Bill Tower on the cot, he knew he had done well; and that in Henry LaTouche's case he could have done no better. He stood at the window, drawing deeply on his cigar, with the faint coolness of the night air drying the sweat on his cheeks. He had that much left, anyhow—a skill that remained untouched. It was something to be grateful for in a world that was crazy beyond calculation. He still was thinking of that an hour later when Bill Tower crawled slowly back from the chloroform's sleep. He went over to Tower and waited until the man's eyes began to center. He said then:

"Your boots are at the foot of the bed. You'll be using them soon enough."

"I had no doubts," murmured Bill, drowsily.

"Gentlemen stick together, Bill."

"What?"

"You did me a favor. I shall try to do you one." He drew a long breath and said, "Stay with him, Charley," and left the room.

Bill Tower turned his head, wistfully. "It was something he said, Charley—and then it was something she said. They're two of a kind."

In the saloon, with his bottle and glass familiarily in front of him, Mark Stanhope remembered Bill Tower's smile. There was something in that to remind him of the gallantry and the courage of the world to which he once had belonged, and from which he now seemed so irretrievably separated. But it was good to know those things still existed. It was like hearing the distant sound of a trumpet on a dark, windy night. Gentlemen stood together. He had one more glass of whisky on that and went out to get his horse.

Riding away from Two Dance it occurred to him that both those people, Bill and Elsa, had a faith that made them stand tall and shapely against the world. It gave them a dignity, it turned them strong and splendid, its presence even

155

seeming to lend him something he had not had before. The footfalls of his pony went ahead of him, for when he rounded Elsa Knightwood's house he saw her standing in the doorway, her supple body against the yellow light, her hair shining in it. He heard her say in a soft, quick way: "Mark." His muscles were heavy and his reactions very slow; when he swung out of the saddle his free foot caught somewhere—and then he pitched headlong into the dust and lay there.

She came running out to him; she dropped on her knees beside him and her arms pulled his heavy shoulders upward. She held him that way, against her breasts. She said: "What have you done!" And she was crying and the faint perfume of her hair was a deep fragrance in this darkness.

"Bill took the fight off my hands and was shot for his kindness. But he will live," he added softly, "to be a man you can put your faith in."

"Mark—Mark!"

This was strange to him. But he had something to say. "You keep thinking of the world you came from. Well, I'm a part of that world—and look at me. It's no good. Forget it. Watch no more trains go through Two Dance. You were not meant to eat your heart out on lost things. You are a full woman, and this Bill Tower would go through fire for you."

She said, all in a rush: "I have reached the end of my strength. I kept thinking I could lean against you for support. You've failed me, Mark! There's nothing in you to help me get my courage back."

He said, all in wonder: "Bill Tower—"

"It isn't kindness I need! It isn't gentleness I need. But why should I have thought that you and I were the same sort?"

He said: "Wait," and tried to get his mind clear. The softness of her body was a comfort to him; her face was dim above him, near as it was. Her arms held his shoulders in a tight, desperate way. He was, he realized bitterly, a failure even in his role of a gentleman returning a favor. He could do Bill Tower no good here. "For a year," he said, "I have watched you come and go. You belong to the world I've been

156

trying to forget. It is why I have kept away from you—until yesterday. But it won't do." His mind was very clear now and his thoughts quite strong, quite lucid. It was like the sensation of a weary man finding a cool spring after long travel across the dry places. He pulled her down and kissed her, and felt the strength of her answer.

SECOND-MONEY MAN

Steve Melody polished the mourners' bench with the seat of his pants, swaying at each pitch of the yonder horse. He planted his feet wider and he punched his hat brim farther back from a grave, dogged face. He said to Bill Tensaw, sitting beside him, "He's makin' that ride look wild and wicked," and he squinted across the arena to where Ray Rand, carried high into the air by the bucking Gray Ghost, cut a splendid silhouette against a background of twenty thousand crazy people in the grandstand. Gray Ghost crashed to the earth on all four stiff feet; dust burst around man and beast, and for the moment there was nothing but Ray Rand's free arm flourishing above this minor maelstrom.

"Fakin' it," criticized Bill Tensaw. "He always does."

"Sure, but swell fakin'."

It was a fact. There was Gray Ghost, which every rider and every judge knew to be a second-rater, and there was Ray Rand, making the crowd believe it to be a terrific struggle. Applause washed over the field as Gray Ghost emerged from the screen of powdered earth and was trapped by the field hands. Ray Rand went out of the saddle, across the rump of a field hand's pony, and struck the earth with an agile spring; he swayed a little and he shook his head, and then he went swiftly over to retrieve his hat and to swing it cheerfully at the stands."

"The weary but conquerin' hero takes his bow," grunted Bill Tensaw. "Rats."

"But he gets 'em," mused Steve. "He sure gets 'em."

"Listen, kid, you can ride circles around Mister Rand and his forty-dollar hat."

"Think so?"

Ray Rand came striding across and stopped at the bench. He took off his hat, recreased it, and placed it on his yellow head at a careful angle. He laid his palms on his hips and grinned down at them.

"I knocked 'em, didn't I? Listen to it."

The Lord had been kind to this man. Fine shoulders swelled up from slim, indented flanks; and his face had a smooth and hungry regularity about it. All his features were mobile, made for quick changes. That grin was something high-hearted and reckless across a bronzed skin. He said again: "Hear 'em holler. Well, we're all washed up for the day."

Steve Melody rose and turned toward the corral gate, the customary way out for contestants, but Ray Rand hooked his arm through Steve's elbow, and drew him around the track so as to pass before the crowd. The day was done, with a late prairie sun casting a higher and higher tide mark on the grandstand roof; field hands ambled wearily across the arena, the crowd was boiling around the exits. Down that long slope somebody yelled, "Good goin', Ray," and Ray Rand whipped his hat outward with a gay carelessness, the grin breaking like sunshine across his cheeks. That gesture Steve Melody had seen repeated a thousand times from Tucson to Calgary, all along the circle.

"Grandstandin'," grunted Steve.

"Why not? What makes the turnstiles click? A hot show. Something that looks like blood. You play to the judges, so you're a second-money man. I play to the crowd, and I pack 'em in."

"Don't bite yourself," said Steve.

"Kid, I did more work than the horse. I'm shot." The smile slid off Rand's face and the corners of his mouth sagged; they went on down the street at a sprawling gait. "After dinner we're going up to see Iris."

"That's a break," muttered Steve.

They were buffeted along Main Street as far as the hotel. In the lobby people stood in solid ranks and at sight of them Ray Rand pulled up his shoulders and smiled again, an actor returning to his role. The inevitable crowd surrounded him. Over in a far corner there was another crowd, through the edges of which he saw the governor of the state; but it made Steve chuckle ironically to see that Ray Rand's audience was larger than the governor's. Showmanship, that was it. Ray's voice, very self-sure, struck through the swelling overtones of talk.

Definitely out of it, Steve Melody went up to his room and stripped, feeling bruised and weary from the tough day. He shaved and he let the hot shower water fall on him till he was groggy; he wrenched on the full cold and sprang out of it with a curdled yell, dripping water all across the room's flowered carpet. He dressed, feeling a little more cheerful, and he sat on the bed and polished his shoes with the end of the bedspread, softly whistling Old Black Joe till he thought of Iris Cantring. Old Black Joe died right there and he held a shoe idle in his big, calloused hands, scowling at the pink-plastered wall.

He hadn't written her a line since he and Ray had left this, their home town, in May to follow the rodeo circuit on the usual summer's competition. She would ask, "Why don't you write to your friends?" And he would have to say that there hadn't been much news, and pull his face together against the search of her quiet, level glance. It was hard to lie to Iris, but less hard than playing an impossible game of friendship with her. Friendship, he thought glumly, was a sad sort of joke when you loved a girl. They had been three wild youngsters on the range, he and Iris and Ray. And then one day the shadow of Ray was between himself and Iris. Ray was always one to get the good things of life, and there was nothing to do but step aside. You don't squawk over bad breaks, you took them and said nothing.

He put on his shoes, fumbling over the laces with his heavy fingers. He drank the water pitcher dry and went down to the jammed dining room and ate his meal at a table for two, faced by a middle-aged woman tourist who seemed inwardly agitated by his presence; a blunt, big-boned man with jet hair shadowing a face inclined to silence and loneliness. An old townsman came by. He said, "You made a swell ride on that General Grant nag," and went away, leaving Steve a little flushed. He couldn't carry it off like Ray.

Old Turk Cantring's house, on the town's highest hill, looked like a stone fort; but it was cool inside, even with the crowd there. An authentic bar ran across one side of the vast living room, ignored by the authorities who wished rodeo week to be in the ancient tradition. Ray Rand drifted off. Somebody handed a glass to Steve, who, after a moment, surreptitiously laid it back on the bar. A voice behind him, serene and amused, caught him in his tracks. "Done in the familiar Melody manner."

He turned exactly on his heels and looked upon an auburn head. Beneath that was a face at once oval and firm and candid—and actually beautiful. The smile seemed to be wholly and wonderfully for him.

"Hello, Iris."

"Why didn't you write?"

"Nothing much to report."

She said, gently: "Maybe I'd think anything from you was news."

"I told Ray to give you my regards when he wrote."

She laid her hand on his solid chest, unsmiling. "It's about time to clear up——"

Ray Rand knifed his way through the people and swung Iris off the floor with his long arms. The blood was running reckless in him, the surrounding sound and warmth had lit the fuse of his mercurial temper. He kissed Iris, laughing at the quick crimson on her cheeks. "Honey," he said, "I been

161

lonesome." Steve Melody felt the glow run out of the night; he felt tired and a little shabby, and he thought, grimly, "Why has the fool got to do that before an audience?"

A slim thing molded in a black dress came up. "I'm collecting curiosities."

"Collect me," Ray Rand drawled.

Iris said: "This is Ray Rand. An old family friend. Helen Vane to you, Ray."

"Hello, honey."

"And Steve Melody."

This Helen Vane's shoulders turned, slowly graceful, and her glance struck Steve. There wasn't much of her, but to him the impression was of live coals burning beneath a smooth, hard surface; of a thoroughly modern creature with red lips across an alert face, and darkly wise eyes classifying him.

"This is that Steve?"

"That one," said Iris.

"What Steve?" interrupted Ray Rand, sharpening interest flicking both girls. An older, iron-haired man came up with fresh glasses. The women refused. Steve refused, courteously. Ray Rand took his glass and held it toward the light. "Good times come again," he said.

Steve reached up, got the glass. "Stick to your trade, sucker. You ride horses."

"Good old watchdog," grinned Ray. One faint trace of irritation licked across the brightness of his eyes.

The gray-haired man said: "Beautiful ride, Rand."

"Thanks, old fellow."

Helen Vane's eyes remained inscrutably on Rand. The older man continued: "Nobody's got it on you—unless it would be Clay Thorp, the greatest of all in his time."

"Yeah," drawled Ray, clipping the words. "He was all right."

Helen Vane's words were faintly malicious: "You like your compliments undiluted."

Iris stirred, changed the subject. "Half the town's here tonight."

162

"Open the doors," said Ray, "and let the other half in."

"You'd like that, too," mused Helen.

Ray's expressive face clouded; his glance locked in hers. Then he was self-sure again. "We'll get along," he drawled.

Iris Cantring moved around, took Steve's arm. "Supposing we ride?"

"Swell," applauded Ray. He pushed back his big hat and reached over and drew Iris away. It was something casually done, like the exercise of a prior right. He whooped for a pathway to the door and pulled the girl on, leaving Steve Melody wooden-cheeked in his tracks. Helen Vane said, carelessly:

"Will I do as a substitute?"

They followed out. Somewhere an orchestra began playing and the floor was a weird scene of jammed couples struggling in their tracks. A giant man with a smile that was a brilliant line against darkly burned skin barred Steve's way briefly at the door. "Take it or leave it, I'm bettin' on you this year." He went on. Ray and Iris were already in the car, Ray racing the motor till sound swelled torrentially down the steet. Steve handed Helen into the back and crawled through. He said irritably to Ray: "In case you don't know, sound is no good without motion," and was flung violently beside the girl as the car shot on.

"Who was that really massive figure back there?" Helen asked.

"Clay Thorp."

She murmured: "Praise from Sir Hubert."

"You can't stop a big fellow from being kind."

"Possibly with reason."

Steve watched Iris Cantring's slim shoulder sway with the motion of the car. They entered the boiling traffic on Main Street. Ray Rand held his fist on the horn and they went blaring recklessly in and out of the jam. It was a fool stunt, Steve thought. "Don't get me wrong," he told the girl. "I'm a second-money man."

"What's that, for heaven's sake?"

"Somewhere above the bum ones, somewhere below the top."

"What a cruel self-analysis."

They were on the dark, level road, the engine roaring full on and the white side-posts flickering by. The square, bold rim of the high country lay black against the steel-colored sky and there was a crystal starlight laying ghostly stripes against the earth. It was at once chilly. Steve remembered the bare, soft shoulders of the girl beside him and squirmed out of his coat. He said, brusquely, "You're a little bit dumb," and draped the coat around her. His hand fell across her shoulders. He saw her straighten and lift her fragrant head near him inquiringly. Sultry irritation pulled his hand back. "No, it wasn't a pass. You been reading a book."

Her voice was a slurred, silken thread: "That's no compliment."

Ray Rand's deep laugh slapped backward and one of his arms lay across the front seat's top, behind Iris, who sat effortlessly still. Steve fumbled at his cigarettes and scratched three matches to make a light. The car caromed along a rutted ditch, screamed around a bend. Steve shouted against the wind: "All right, Oldfield, turn back. There's a rodeo tomorrow."

They went about, town lights throwing yellow flares against the velvet black. Ray Rand began singing to himself. Helen's shoulder lay comfortably against Steve; her talk was almost severe: "Loyalty's all right. But don't be blind."

"Which way does that cut?"

Her laugh was soft and full. She said, aloud: "You're right, Iris." Ray Rand's tone was deeply ironic over his shoulder. "The man's made of metal, honey. Don't bother with him." But Iris Cantring had turned and Steve saw her smiling at him through the dark. They crossed the railroad tracks, rolled squalling through town again, to the hotel. The men got out. Steve went around and stood with one foot on the running board, near Iris, whose hand came out and held him there. A long shadow ran across her face and she spoke, only for his ears:

"I want to see you tomorrow. I want to see *you* alone, do you understand?" Steve took off his hat, glance passing back to the others. Helen Vane was coolly matching Ray Rand's suddenly intent inspection. She was playing with him, Steve thought irritably, and very sure of herself. But he knew better. That was one game Ray Rand never lost.

Iris Cantring's abruptly dug-in grip startled him. She said, suppressed and tense: "You blamed fool, why don't you think more of yourself? Why don't you fight your own battles instead of somebody else's? You're not a second-money man, you idiot! If you only saw yourself right you wouldn't be second to anybody—in anything! Anything, do you hear?"

Utterly astonished, he saw the blaze of temper color her cheeks, turn alive the vigor of her serene features. She looked as though she wanted to swear at him; she looked exactly as he had seen her sometimes look in her tomboy days, outraged and ready to cry. She said, "You never did take care of yourself, Steve Melody," put the car in gear and shot away, leaving him coatless and bemused in the street.

He clapped on his hat, muttered, "What the hell?" And he walked through the lobby in his shirt, a pair of red sleeve-holders screeching at the world. In his room he opened windows and transom. Noise poured through, a festival-inclined people roamed along the hotel corridors. He felt dry and drawn—the aftermath of a sweaty day—and he drank six glasses of tepid water from the tap. He took off his shirt and hung it around the back of a chair; he stuffed his socks in his shoes, put the shoes under the bed. Stripped to undershirt and pants he padded down the hall to the adjoining room. Ray lay full length on the bed. There were two empty ginger-ale bottles on the table and three empty glasses. The place reeked.

"Give yourself a break, sucker."

Ray sat up. "I got 'er made, kid."

"Get in bed, you dumb bunny."

"There's a couple guys here from Hollywood. This has been on fire for a month. It's all settled. As soon as I knock over the trophy day after tomorrow we sign. A year in pictures."

"Pictures?"

"Horse opera, kid. I got what they want."

Steve borrowed a cigarette from the table. He scowled at the empty glasses, dragged down a deep draught of smoke. "What've you got they want, sonny boy?"

"I knock 'em, don't I? Is that an accident? I play this game for all the angles. I put on a show. I go over. I always was headed for pictures. I'm in, see?"

"You punish the bubble water any more and you ain't in no place, sucker." Steve snapped out the lights. "For a big guy you sure show weak moments. Get the hell in bed before I work on you."

"Not sore, kid?"

"Nope."

This was the second day, with a hard sunlight drenching the arena and dust smell strong in the nostrils and twenty thousand people howling for anything short of murder. The loudspeakers had flung his name to every corner of the arena: "Steve Melody on Jupe Pluvius." Steve went into the saddle and kicked his feet solidly through the stirrups. He rubbed the dampness out of his palms, gave a last yank to his hat and took hold of the hackamore. A little hush crossed the field. Steve murmured, "Another day, another dollar." The field hand said, "You can have the dollar, kid," and let go of snub rope and blind.

Jupe Pluvius went up, the feeling like that of being hurled at the sky. The horse's big muscles swelled between Steve's legs and his head swooped gauntly down. The earth rose violently to meet them, a series of shocks passed through bone and leather, and ground Steve's vertebrae into the separating cartilage. Steve thought, remote and lonely on this hurricane seat, "The horse is all right, and I'm all right," and then his thinking was submerged in a fluid calm that controlled nerve and muscle.

Jupe Pluvius strained onward out of the pillowed dust of his own making, into the fire-bright sunlight; Jupe Pluvius shook a maddened head and reared, front feet striking the air; and came down with an enraged effort. Steve's bat-wing chaps cracked bitterly, his chest telegraphed pain from belly to shoulder blades; and afterward the horse exploded in a stiff, four-footed leaping that sledged the man at each landing. Steve heard a dim roaring. On the heels of a faint report from afar two field hands cut through the battle smoke and seized the horse's head. It was all over. Steve went over the left pick-up man's horse and hit the ground awkwardly.

The roaring struck him in the face; up in the stands white and crimson clothing churned vividly. Steve moved on at a spraddling walk, retrieved his hat; there was a great deal of humbleness in him, and a faint bitterness. "The second-money man must have put on a show," he thought and turned through the corral gate. He sat on a bale of hay, heavy arms idle on his thighs.

A big man tramped out of the arena and stopped and looked down, a grin broadening across a swart bronze. "Kid," Clay Thorp drawled, " it was a ride!" and went back. Then, looking up, Steve saw Iris and Helen Vane.

"The Thinker, with more clothes on," murmured Helen, and moved quietly aside. Iris came on until her trim, square shoulders faced Steve. A faint flow of color touched her oval cheeks, and something disturbed the honesty of her straight glance.

"Ray's up on Picketwire," Steve said. "You'll miss a good ride."

"I saw a good ride."

"I had a little luck."

"This," she murmured, "is going to be difficult."

He stood steady, puzzled. A thick wave of applause leaped the arena wall and broke about them. "Let old Doctor Melody fix you up," he said.

"Steve—what's the idea in general?"

"Come again, Iris."

"Don't be dumb. You're not."

"Listen, Iris, we've grown up. This brother and sister stuff won't go."

"So you sent your best wishes by Ray. There was a time . . . Answer me this: Whoever told you that Ray and I—"

Ray Rand, walked up, an eager, alert glance beneath the reckless rake of his hat. It was, Steve thought, like a strong wind running across sultriness. But there was something strange here. Ray walked toward Iris and then the girl's parasol made a seemingly idle semicircle along the dust in front of her. It stopped Ray. He said, dryly: "Shyness becomes you, honey."

"Something new under the sun to you, Mr. Rand?" purred Helen Vane.

"What's the shootin' for?" drawled Ray. But Steve saw his eyes go coolly speculative against the girl. Steve swung away, hot fury in him. He passed down a stable's alley and out the far end; he crossed a corral, saw Ray and the girls idling toward an exit. He let himself through a turnstile and tramped back to the hotel. It was a crazy world. You had what the crowd wanted or you didn't. If you had it, everything was yours for the asking. If you didn't have it, you were just another mug walking home from a day's work with the crowd digging you in the ribs. What was the matter with the yellow-haired fool that, having one fine girl, he had to go lushing all around the map?

Coming along the hall at eight o'clock, he stopped abruptly by Ray Rand's door. Full light glowed over the transom and a crisp voice said one quick phrase and turned silent. Steve wheeled. He said "Sucker" glumly, and marched unannounced into the room. Helen Vane stood poised against a wall, a striking picture, and watched Ray pour a drink. Rand's head tilted and he spilled liquor over the table. Plain annoyance licked across his cheeks.

"Kid," he said, "what's a door for?"

"For misplaced little girls to walk out of," said Steve. Helen rose. "The man means it, bless him."

"Wait," called Ray Rand. "I don't get this straight. Where do you live?"

"An address for your card index?" mocked the girl.

"And," said Steve, "the curfew is ringin'."

"Peaceably, officer."

Steve followed her to the hall. He shut the door, leaned wearily against it. Helen Vane's voice was husky, faintly amused: "I never have been bounced before, but I recognize the hand of an expert."

"Might be something in that."

"And so you learned about women from him?"

He said, impassively: "No soap."

"But you hate a cheater."

There was something baffling about her. She stood before him, frank and vivid-lipped, like so many others who had drifted toward the brilliant light of Ray Rand's personality; yet her eyes were different—unsoiled in their gray depths. She said: "For no reason at all I wish you didn't think that of me. I told you once I collected specimens. Now go back and guard your great man."

He retreated into the room. Ray said, aggrievedly: "I wish to God you'd keep out of my affairs."

"For a big guy you're soft as mush."

"Kid, I'll get along."

"Soft as mush! Listen, sucker, I've bailed gals out of your rooms all the way from Caliente to Calgary. What the heck ails you—pickin' a cheap skirt right in front of Iris?"

"Melody—the big moral influence."

"Yeah? Anyhow, I'm no gyp."

"I'm a gyp?" Ray Rand's mouth thinned. "I take too much from you, kid." But he quit scowling. He moved his hands placatingly. "Quit it. I wouldn't hurt Iris for a million. It's on the up and up. This Helen just crashed it. Could I help it?"

"Yes."

Rand sat on the bed, rubbing his head. "Something serious

here. About me and tomorrow. I need the championship to-morrow to clinch the bargain. No trophy, no flicker-flicker contract. I ride Deception. Not much of a fighter, but I'll make a show."

"Sure."

Rand threw his question bluntly across the room: "You realize it's you and me and Ott Lewes in the finals?"

Steve studied that. Surprise touched his cheeks.

"I'd never given it a tumble. A fact, ain't it? Old second-money man went and sneaked among high-class folks."

"Lewes is out. Not enough points even if he makes a good ride. But you're hot, and we're actually square on points. I've figured it. You drew the best bucker."

"Afraid of me?" said Steve, grinning his disbelief.

"You're hot. You're ridin' away over your head this week."

"Thanks, sucker, for the left-handed approval."

Ray Rand rose and turned over to the windows, seeming to look out. He spoke over his shoulder: "Kid, don't make too good a ride tomorrow."

Steve put his hand on the table. He got a cigarette, tapped it, he held it between his fingers and slowly rolled it shape-less, a bleak blue in his eyes. Ray wheeled and spoke rapidly: "Who gives the crowd a kick? Who packs the stands? Who's box office in this game? Me—Ray Rand. If I wasn't riding, half those seats would be empty. All right. Here you come, clear outside your ability, to make it tough for me just when I'm lookin' at money. I ought to get the break, kid. It belongs to me."

Steve pushed the table half an inch forward. He shoved the water bottle to the center of it, set the cigarette pack neatly on its bottom. He went out without looking back, hearing Ray call swiftly, "I've done a lot for you." In his room, he undressed, scuffed around the carpet with his bare feet, rugged head canted downward.

"This is the guy," he said, spuriously gentle, "I thought was a great man. This is the guy I been wet-nursin' four years. What a hell of a tumble I'm takin'! And that's the mug Iris wants."

The loudspeakers announced him: "Steve Melody on Skulduggery." He got the field hand's signal and stepped forward and went into the saddle at one surge. Ott Lewes had ridden and lost; Ray Rand was yet to ride; and here he was, Steve Melody, second-money man, seated high and stark before twenty thousand people on a midnight-black beast racked with rage in each sprung muscle.

"You got a horse, kid," said the field hand.

He felt stripped, inexpressibly lonely. It was one thing to be part of the pack, making a good living in an unnoticed way; it was another thing to sit in the middle of a bright field, the target of the world. Out of the ruck he had come after four years of drudging, to command all this attention, to have the interest of the crowd burning into him for the space of one brief minute. The feeling was something new, something that ruffled along the back of his neck like cold wind, that sliced into him and swelled his lungs and turned his stomach cold. He seated his boots in the stirrups, felt the horse flatten and harden. From the corners of his eyes he saw the field hands fade. There was one long moment of suspense. Afterwards Skulduggery broke in the middle and sunfished into the dry, golden light.

It came to him then, flashing through an unmoved corner of his mind. This was what the top riders felt—this nerveless certainty. This was what made them grin at the world. This was what he always saw in their eyes—an iron pride. Skulduggery crashed down, shuddering from his own punishment. Flame streaked across Steve's eyeballs. Something seemed to burst. But it was like riding the wind and having no fear. He met and matched the violent pitching, muscles loose, brain alert, that wonderful sense of mastery fresh and strong in him.

Far back in the saddle he caught the arriving detonations as they beat up through Skulduggery and wrung the long muscles of his back bitterly; the ligaments of his vitals felt it, a black cloud rushed through his head. And there was then an indescribable feeling of the earth turning crazy, followed

171

by a cessation of motion. Through the acrid pall he saw the pick-up men holding the horse's head.

He went off and landed flatfooted, the impact knocking his teeth together. He stood still, vertigo tossing him. Clay Thorp's black visage, creased by that dazzling smile, looked out of blankness. "I saw you comin' two years ago. You're here."

Steve muttered, "Thanks, old boy," and went for his hat. He turned sharp, went spraddling toward the corral gate. A great, round "Oh" breathed from the crowd and he swung his head in time to see Ray Rand, up on Deception, go askew and fall like a vagrant shadow. Ray struck the ground hard, rolled on and on; he came clawing to his feet, made a complete turn. One long arm punched enraged blows at the stands, a crazy, unreasoning, unforgivable thing; and then he whipped about and charged at the corral gate.

"Kid," said Steve, gently, "it's tough luck."

Ray Rand scarcely stopped. Yellow temper sheeted from his eyes. "You damned ingrate!" he yelled. "I ought to kill you!" Afterwards he vanished into the dark alley of a stable.

Steve ambled as far as a little splash of sunlight against the arena wall; and he halted there, soaking up the heat, strangely stirred and strangely saddened. It was funny, but all affection was gone and what remained now was cruel knowledge. The greatness of Ray Rand had died; a part of himself had died with it. No other man would ever again mean the same to him.

A voice said: "Somewhere the spotlight of fame is shining for you, Steve."

Helen Vane had come up. There was, he thought, irony in the words, but her eyes were softer and brighter than he remembered. "I don't know why most bad men are wise about women and most good men so blind. Whoever told you Iris loved him?"

"I knew it long ago."

"Did Iris ever tell you?"

"No," he said. "No-o."

172

"Don't you know his kind of a man wants an option on all the good things of the world? Just an option to take up or throw aside. Anything to keep others away. Why do you suppose I was in his room? Hoping you'd see what he was, of course. I told you I collected specimens. Well, he was a poor one. I knew that in the beginning. So did Iris. Hasn't she been trying to tell you? Oh, Steve, you idiot!"

The loudspeakers were calling him. He leaned forward. "Why, Helen?"

"Just a girl scout," she said softly, bitterly. "Iris is my friend."

"I was dead wrong about you."

"That's a break," she said, and turned her back to him swiftly. Steve went into the stable and got his horse; and rode through the corral gate to get the silver trophy in front of twenty thousand people.

He came into the hotel at six, surreptitiously, through a side door. Skulking up the stairs, he passed a woman, an utter stranger, who smiled at him and suddenly put a paper in his hands and went on, laughing. Halted there, his eyes met this, in black type: "Out of the unknown today an iron man by the name of Steve Melody emerged to furnish the most thrilling climax known to round-up history. Unsung and unheralded, Melody stepped up on the outlaw bucker, Skulduggery. Fifteen seconds later a new champion was born. The intervening time was a scene unforgettable. This rawboned, granite-souled man, with the shock of black hair falling down across a dogged face that would delight a scupltor, had drama and color in his very fingertips—"

He said "Stuff!" and threw the paper behind him. He walked into the hall. He stopped, a faint, glinting grin on his cheeks; and then he entered Rand's room.

"About this ingrate business, sucker—"

Ray Rand laid a whisky glass carefully on the table and took two rapid steps forward. "You came after it, huh?" he yelled. And he laced out with one wild swing. Steve Melody's grin sharpened. His broad, fending palm absorbed the blow harmlessly and his own right fist crashed into the drawn face before him, utterly destroying the expression on it. And that was all.

Rand went backward, seizing the edge of the table as he collapsed. The table went over on top of him and the water bottle fell and cracked in a dozen pieces.

"Kid," said Steve, "your publicity fooled me. I thought you were as great as they said you were. Now they're sayin' it about me—and I know it's all a lie."

He went out, big lungs drawing a little faster, the odd smile remaining. He shifted his tie and pushed open his own door—and teetered on his toes. Iris Cantring rose from the depths of a chair, like an image of comfort to a weary traveler in the desert. She had on a ruffled dress that made her square shoulders seem squarer; and she was looking at him as he never expected any woman could. She said, calmly enough:

"I hear you object to strange women in men's rooms—"

"I suppose," he reflected, "I've got to play up to what I'm supposed to be. Apparently you can make your own rules when the world's your oyster. Well, I know another car and another road . . ."

"Steve, what does a girl have to do? I have thrown everything at you but the state militia. You'll never better your chances standing clear across the room."

He said, moving forward, "The good things of life come slowly."

THE OUTCAST

Noon found the wagon train in a dry and destitute country broken by shallow ridges whose mica-crushed slopes glittered in the sunlight. The four parallel columns of the train came to a ponderous stop and were immediately enveloped by a dense, sparkling fog of alkali dust; families gathered in the scant lee shade of the wagons to eat and to rest while the herd of loose stock, under guard, began a drifting search for the scorched and scattered grass tufts. Springtime and the green, flat miles of the Platte were far behind; between this point and Oregon lay a thousand miles of country rougher than these travelers had so far seen.

The quick meal done, certain young men began to stroll out from the wagons to make a group by themselves, to sit and smoke and talk. There were a dozen such footloose lads who, wanting the adventure of this journey and the free land westward, but being penniless, had hired out to drive the extra wagons of the train.

It was one of these, Til McLean, who first spotted the rising puffs of dust behind the nearest ridge. "Well," he said, "there they come again," and he rolled over on an elbow to watch a small party of Indians—ten of them, the count turned out—come to the crest of the ridge on their ragged horses, and jog down upon the train.

Their approach caused no commotion; the emigrants were wiser now than they had been at first sight of the Sioux, many days back. Since then it was a common thing to have these bands come in to talk or beg or steal, usually civil, but

175

always with the surly gleaming of resentment quite plain in their eyes. This particular band passed the group of young men and continued to the head of the wagons, where the train captain would be.

Ben Ash said, "Same band that's been hangin' on our flank for a week. Still tryin' to make us pay for the privilege of goin' through their country."

"The privilege ain't worth much," said Til McLean. He was a lank and travel-tattered young man, his ragged mass of blond hair seeming lighter still against the weather stain on his face; his neck and shoulders and chest were large, and his gray eyes, restless with deviltry, closely followed the Indians and watched them go into a palaver with the captain and a few older men.

"I wonder what's up?" Ben Ash said.

"Go see," said Til McLean.

"I will," said Ben Ash, and rose and went up the wagon line. After a short time he rejoined the group grinning, and said, "The fellow with the big nose is a chief, he says. He wants to buy a white girl for a squaw."

"Why, now," said Til McLean, "we've got barely enough for ourselves." But the idea of it made him smile, and the urge to raise a little fun began to work within him.

He saw Abbie Dickson halfway up the line, staring at the Indians with a hand shading her eyes, and the idea grew greater. He sat upright, chuckling, and idly drew cross marks on the ground.

Captain Whitney, at length growing weary of the situation, said a few words and waved his hands. This, after being interpreted by Fitzpatrick, turned the Indians about and sent them down the line of wagons.

Til McLean rose, his eyes glittering with amusement, but he erased the expression, imitating the wooden nothingness on the faces of the Indians coming forward. He put up a hand to stop the leading Indian and twisted a forefinger through the air, pointing back to Abbie Dickson. The Indian swung to give the girl a thorough inspection and returned his attention to Til McLean, who again pointed to the girl and afterward tapped his own chest.

"Mine. My squaw. For twenty horses"—and he laid his extended fingers twice against the air—"she's your squaw. Twenty." He pointed to Abbie, to himself, and at last to the Indian.

The Indian's eyes stayed on Til McLean, neither winking nor wavering. He spoke to the Indian nearest him, and got an answer. He held up ten fingers. McLean shook his head and his ten fingers again rose twice. The Indian made another appraisal of Abbie Dickson, gave a short grunt, and the whole group rushed away.

It was a situation that amused all the young men, and puzzled a few of them.

Ben Ash said, "Think you made a sale?"

"Bet he comes back with twenty horses," said Til.

"Hell to pay if he does," said Ben Ash. "Abbie will take a gun to you."

Hub Pickett said, "Last time it was a skunk under Sarah Crocker's washtub. She ain't been able to wash in it since."

"A little fun's no harm," said Til.

As the bugle signalled for renewed march, McLean reached Captain Whitney's second wagon near the head of the third column and climbed to the seat. Whitney's daughter, Alice, appeared presently at the foot of the near wheel. McLean reached for her arm and helped her to the seat possessively.

She was seventeen, of a round, full, woman's shape within her clothes, the calmness of her disposition mirrored by a pleasant and practical face. In the sixty days of riding together on this wagon seat they had gone through a quiet courtship and had reached an understanding, thinking it was still a secret affair.

She said, "I heard. Why did you pick on Abbie Dickson? You put out with her?"

"No."

"Because she's the prettiest?"

"No, I just happened to see her standing there. Will she be mad about it?"

"She'll think you're interested in her."

"I never meant that," he said, and was momentarily taken aback. "I meant nothing. It just got into my head, something to make a litle fuss in a long day. It was only a joke."

The bugle spoke again, the columns groaned into tedious forward motion and the herders rounded the loose stock into traveling shape behind the column, men and animals soon lost within the furious clouds of dust.

Alice Whitney pulled her bonnet tighter, but this was a useless gesture against the dust which was everywhere. The big wagon wheels bailed it up and poured it back like sheets of water, and it rose again in creamy turbulence to coat every flat surface, to clog nostrils and sink into lungs, to paint every face an ash gray, to sink through clothing and become a gritty discomfort against damp skin. The girl lightly touched her cheek and thereafter put her hands on her lap, deliberately keeping upon her face an expression of patience.

At four o'clock a band of Indians showed on the ridge to their right and ran forward with a herd of horses making a minor thunder before them.

Til McLean's eyes turned, widened, and a delighted smile came upon his face. "He swallowed the bait."

Alice Whitney's "Oh, dear," was a soft and worried sigh.

The wagons came to their awkward halt while Captain Whitney and his lieutenants moved out to meet the Indians a hundred yards from the column; then Whitney and Fitzpatrick rode forward and one of the Indians rode forward. The Indian, having preserved a moment's dignified silence, spoke, made a motion toward the horses he had brought, and pointed at the train. Whitney said a word which Fitzpatrick translated. From his seat on the wagon, Til McLean watched the exchange grow sharper. The Indian was insistent. McLean looked across the gap to the wagon in the adjoining column and saw Ben Ash's grin come back.

"I said he would, didn't I?" said McLean.

"He did," said Ben Ash, and fell into a great laugh.

Captain Whitney, finding diplomacy futile against the Indian's stubborn attitude, suddenly cut his hand definitely through the air. The Indian lifted his fist to the sky, brought it slowly downward, and shook it at the column. Then he wheeled and led his band and his horses rapidly over the ridge and out of sight.

"Til," said Alice Whitney, "he's mad."

"Serves him right," said McLean cheerfully. "Been bothering us a week. Maybe now he'll quit."

Captain Whitney came straight through the wagons, Fitzpatrick with him, to where McLean sat. The captain was in his early fifties. A fringe of gray-white whiskers along chin and jaw borders gave him a certain air of kind dignity; the dense gray coloring of his eyes lent a resolute touch to his character—and these two things, appealing to the people of the wagon train, had elected him captain. He sat well on a horse, he was grave enough to consider, and brisk enough to command. Now, speaking to McLean, he maintained a considerate tone and expressed no particular feeling, but his daughter knew how deeply angered he was.

"Til," he said, "you made the dicker with that savage?"

McLean's smile diminished. "I thought we'd have a little fun."

"In his mind you made a bargain with him. I had to break it, which is to him bad faith. It also got at his pride, and that offends him most."

"Well," said McLean easily, "with a hundred men in this train and a lot of good rifles, he'll have to swallow his pride. It will do him no good." Then he added, "I meant nothing by it."

Whitney said, "If you meant nothing, you should have said nothing. I must tell you it was foolish. This train has kept out of trouble by offering no offense. There are too many people in it to be put to the risk of one man's carelessness."

McLean sat still, Whitney's words were loud enough to carry to the other nearby wagons where people listened, and Alice was here to hear it, and the guide's taciturn face stared at him with no compliment upon it. He was a young man caught up in the consequences of an impulse, having no reasonable excuse, knowing what poor ground he stood on, and more and more resentful that it should be pointed out to him before witnesses. He said shortly, "Nothing will happen."

Whitney's tone was dry. "I join you in the hope."

For a moment he continued to watch McLean, reading the younger man's face. But it was clear that McLean did not comprehend the possible seriousness of his act. He felt he had been unduly blamed and thus he was still not a man of thoughtfulness. Captain Whitney turned away with the guide.

McLean sat with a sultry silence wrapping him around. The girl, seeing this, touched him with her hand and loyally put herself on his side. "He was wrong to make it sound so bad. Older people always get too sober about things. Don't you mind."

He remained uncomforted. "Any man in the train might have done the same thing. There's nothing to worry about. Nothing's going to happen. It was only a joke. Everybody laughed about it, didn't they?"

As night fell, the long-practiced columns went wheeling into one great circle until the big wagons and their tough canvas sides made the walls of a round fort, inside which the camp would be sheltered; fires rose from the earth at a hundred places, brightly breaking the lamp-black shadows; skillets and dutch ovens made their clanging racket; and the smell of coffee soon came. The tedious business of preparing a camp completed, quiet settled over the train. A fiddle's music drew one group together, a guitar and a singer drew another. Small children ducked in and out of the leaping light, mysterious with their games, while young men and women carelessly drifted into pairs and faded from view.

Sitting beside his fire, Captain Whitney saw Alice and Til McLean disappear, he saw his oldest daughter move past the Halsey fire and draw Ferg Halsey away without a turn of her head. His lieutenants came by and spoke a minute and went on.

Then, knowing that a captain alone and aloof was a poor captain, he rose to make his round of the fires. These people respected his judgment, but Captain Whitney was a politician who understood that leadership depended more on the touch of one human being against another than all the wisdom in creation. And so he passed along the fires, dropping his pleasant words, hearing a complaint and answering it with a thoughtful nod, speaking a little and listening much. Peace enveloped the camp in the stillness of the night.

Then he heard the sharp instrusion of a herder's voice into this quiet, a quick cry of alarm and challenge, and hard after it the flat bursting of a gun. The cry caught on until it was a general alarm, more guns speaking. A woman within the camp corral screamed and men reared from the earth and rushed through the wagon gaps toward the growing confusion of guns and voices.

Captain Whitney ran for his wagon and got his gun. Once beyond the line of wagons, he realized how flimsy their preparation for this contingency had been; the long lectures on military order and discipline might as well not have been given. Blackness and disorder were everywhere. There was no center to the fight and no way of knowing white man from Indian.

Guns blazed away, their muzzle flashes dotting the dense shadows; an occasional stray arrow—the Indians were using both bows and guns— struck the thick canvas of the wagon covers with a whacking report. His men were shouting, but making little sense, while the barking coyote cry of the Indians whirled in from all points.

Captain Whitney lifted his fullest voice into the bedlam. "Men! All come here!" It was a futile try. He could not make himself heard. And thus stripped temporarily of leadership by the confusion, he stood helpless, bitterly absorbing the

181

lesson many a captain had learned on the battlefield: drill and reality were two separate things.

It was a quick and clever attack, lasting but a short while. Captain Whitney launched his call into the descending calm. "Come up here. Gather by me! Come now, run up, run up!"

His scattered men moved in from every compass point.

"Now, then," he said, "you men on horse, ride out there fast. They didn't get all the animals. Get out there quick and round up all the saddle stock you can find. Bring it here. You fellows on foot, get your saddles and wait by me until the horses come in. Saddle and go out. Start working the stray animals in. Hurry now. Get on there."

Immediately, half a dozen voices came at him with conflicting advice. He recognized Tom Whitson's, who said: "Never mind the strays. We'll get the horses and make a chase after those damned savages. They can't drive oxen fast. They won't be far ahead. We'll get 'em back."

Captain Whitney then and there demonstrated he was something more than a man to listen and to console. He struck hard at the suggestion. "That's what they want—to pull us from the wagons so they can hit. It won't do. First thing's to get the stock. Get out there boys, and bring in the horses."

He listened to the riders splash over the creek and run away. Then he heard George Dickson shout: "That Til McLean, I'm going to kill him!"

"No, you won't," said Captain Whitney. "We'll settle that later, but you'll fire no gun at anybody here. Some of you men go out and see if anybody's hurt."

Riders began to come in with extra horses, and these were at once saddled and ridden back into the night.

Whitney said, "Bring in the nearest stuff first. Make a wider sweep each time, but don't go out yonder alone. Bunch up when you hunt beyond half a mile. Drive everything back here and right inside the wagons. Boys, move Letcher's wagon out of the way so we'll have a gate. Anybody found hurt yet?"

Nobody had been killed or hurt. "Well," he said dryly,

"they ain't no better at shooting than we are. Til, are you here?"

Til McLean's voice came from the edge of the group, short and quiet. "Here."

"Well," said Captain Whitney, "stay by where you can hear me when I call you."

Dickson spoke again. "I tell you, McLean, if I see you I'll kill you."

"That will do, George," said Captain Whitney. "Everybody inside the line of wagons. Build up those fires so we can count the stock when it comes in."

He called his lieutenants forward. "Put some young men out there on the north side. We're not watching sharp enough. Taggart, I want you to keep an eye on Dickson. I'll have no shooting. The train couldn't survive it."

He counted the oxen as they came through and was, for a little while, hopeful. These animals, too slow and too weary to stampede well, had lagged and had been left behind by the Indians. Toward the end of an hour he tallied ninety of the beasts returned, ninety out of two hundred; then the strays dwindled to single ones brought from afar. Near midnight, the searchers returned from a final sweep and Whitney called a meeting at his campfire.

"We have recovered a hundred and six. The rest are gone or dead. We have teams enough for fifty-three wagons. The other forty-seven will have to be abandoned."

The people of the train made a great ring around him, frozen into silence by the brutal loss they had sustained, and by the hard thoughts which came of it. He saw the shadowy shapes of the women in the background, all the young men in their own group; they had drifted toward Til McLean and stood with him to give him their speechless support. It was the old against the young, he thought, the division ancient and forever sharp.

Tom Whitson spoke from the shadows, "We'll make up a party in the morning and chase after those Indians."

Captain Whitney, expecting such a suggestion, had given it long thought while counting the stock in and now made his well-formed answer. "It won't work. They're a long way off by now. If they saw us coming they'd butcher the oxen anyhow. But the main thing is, we've not got men enough to go on a chase and guard this train at the same time. There's no way of knowing how many of those creatures are squatted over the hill waiting for us to be foolish. There is only one thing to do. We have got to crowd everything into fifty-three wagons. Bedding and food and clothes. Everything else must be left—furniture, all your fancy stuff."

"Whose wagons go, whose are left behind?" asked Dickson.

Captain Whitney said, "Those that have saved their oxen will take their wagons. The rest will double up—except those that had more than one wagon. If their extra oxen are here, these men will give the beasts to a man who has none."

The circle broke and Whitney walked toward his own outfit. Somebody shouted, "Look out," and a rifle went off and he turned to see George Dickson struggling against the interference of two other men.

Dickson, having lost team and wagon, could not restrain his anger. "By God, McLean, I will not rest until I do it." McLean stood in his tracks, never having moved from his original place.

Whitney said, "Be still, George. We will settle that matter as soon as we're fixed up." He went on to his wife, to face her and to see the misery in her eyes.

"Must we lose so much, Whitney? Can't I take my mother's dishes?"

"No," he said. His oldest daughter came up. He said, "Bedding, clothes and food. We'll go in with the Halseys." He looked for his other daughter, wanting her help at this chore, but he saw her with Til McLean and he had not the heart to call her.

Whitney went heavily to his labors. When all their things had been stowed into the Halsey wagon he observed that the little mounds had grown into one huge mound in the center of the circle.

"Bring up the teams," he called.

The oxen were yoked, the emptied wagons pulled together and left there. The packed wagons, forming line, wheeled into a new circle farther along the creek. It was then two in the morning and suddenly, against the black night sky, one great flame rose from the old camp, brightening the shadows of the new camp until half a daylight lay over it. Women were freely crying when he sent his call across the compound. "We'll hold our meeting now."

"Whitney," said his wife, "you know the boy's to be your son-in-law."

"There ought not to be much kindness in you for him," he said. "Your mother's things are burning."

"It's Alice I think about," she said. "How many people have you got to make suffer?"

He was about to answer, but was stopped by a warning motion of his wife's hand and, turning, he saw Alice coming swiftly forward, her face so drawn that it seemed to be scarred. She said to him, "You can talk for him. You've got to talk for him."

He shook his head. "I've got to talk for the camp. Alice, not for him," he said and turned into the waiting circle. "Til, come here."

For a moment, he had the fear that the young man might have slipped away during the changing of camp, and it pleased him to see how promptly Til McLean came into the circle to face him. It was, Whitney thought, a showing of honesty that would help the boy with his judges.

"Now, then," said Whitney, "shall he be punished, or has he had enough?"

Ben Ash spoke at once, expressing the common thought of the younger men. "What's the good of carrying it on? I'd guess he's sorrier for it than he could say if he talked all night. Why make it worse on a man who's got no way of turnin' the clock back to make it different? We all thought it was funny when he did it."

An unknown voice, more exhausted than angry, came from the shadows. "I didn't. There's nothin' funny about monkeyin' with Indians, any time."

"Well," said Ben Ash, "we all did. It just came up, like you'd turn over your hand. Nothing meant by it, nothin' expected of it."

George Dickson's voice rushed into the argument, intemperate now as it had been earlier. "One more joke like that will be the end of us. It was the act of a fool, and we can stand no more fools. Forty-seven families in this train have got no oxen, no wagons. Neither will they have plows or harness or tools or crocks. Neither will any of us have food to carry us though the first winter in Oregon. All for the act of a fool. You want mercy for a thing like that? I don't. I say we've got to get rid of him before he does it again, to leave our bones bleach out here. If he's alive around here tomorrow, I'll shoot him. That's my word on it."

Ben Ash's retort went angrily back to Dickson. "Then, by God, I'll shoot you and you'll have a bellyfull of shootin'."

"That's plenty of that," said Captain Whitney, and waited for more talk. When it failed to come he looked at Til McLean.

"If it's on your mind to speak, now's the time."

McLean said, "Those Indians have been trailing us for a week. Suppose I'd not started the joke—can you be sure we wouldn't have been hit anyhow?"

George Dickson's strident voice rose at once. "Answer your own question. What do you think?"

There was a long delay, in which Captain Whitney found himself waiting with more than usual interest for the answer. It came out with a straightness that again pleased him. "I don't know," said McLean.

"There you are," retorted Dickson, and fell silent.

"I will want a show of hands on this," said Captain Whitney slowly. "Is he to be punished? All for it lift up." He saw the hands rise against the darkness all around the circle

186

save the one spot where the younger men stood. He made his estimated count. "All against it," he said, and watched far fewer hands lift. He said quietly, "I must say that it's four to one in favor." He held his tone to its same even level. "What shall the punishment be?"

Time grew later and exhaustion worked its way with these people. The first vote had let out some of the violent anger within them, and the silence now grew long. He feared it would be Dickson who first broke it but instead, the unknown voice came again with its weary, unrelenting gentleness.

"Cap'n, what would you do with him?"

Whitney said, "You want me to name it?"

"I'd abide it."

The captain's first thought was of McLean—this man who was not yet a full man, mirroring by his strong streak of deviltry the restlessness of all the young ones. Perhaps, in this affair, he had learned his lesson, for certainly he had stood up to the camp well and had made but one excuse; yet in that excuse there was the shadow of doubt, the small tone of a pride not quite convinced, of a willfulness not yet subdued. If that were the case, this boy needed a greater shock, to kill him as a fool or to season him into wisdom.

But what of the train? He knew these people well, their endurance, their goodness, their passions, their cranky democracy. Equality was their god, and they would level him quicker than any other man, simply because they had placed him higher. There was but one decision. Any other would destroy the hard-bought harmony of the train. It would crack the train apart and leave it as a collection of weak fragments straggling across a thousand miles of empty land. . . . He lifted his head, knowing he had been long still.

"Dent, will you get my saddle under Halsey's wagon and saddle my tan mare yonder by Kirby's wagon?" On the far edge of the group he saw his wife and his daughter. "Alice, you catch up a muslin sack. Put in it a side of bacon, five pounds of flour, a hand of salt and sugar, a bit of coffee." The great fire around the burning wagons leaped far into the sky, turning this scene bright. He looked at Til McLean. "In ten minutes you'll take that outfit and leave this train. Don't come back."

And in the heavy silence of anger satisfied and vengeance exacted, he sensed the pity the crowd could now afford to give a young man about to set out on a journey across the leagues of an inhospitable earth. Within the circle of these wagons there was safety; beyond, there was none. He searched the circle to find the guide.

"Fitz, you have ten minutes to tell this boy how to stay alive."

Fitzpatrick took but half the time, never a man to pile on words. Then McLean turned and walked toward the line of wagons where Alice stood, and the two disappeared behind a wagon.

The crowd hung on, weary as it was, waiting for the end of it. Bill Dent brought up the saddled tan mare, the muslin sack of grub tied behind. Captain Whitney looked at his watch, saw it was two-thirty, and stared at the sky for the first stain of morning. His bones were like crumbling sticks, his flesh a-creep with fatigue, his spirit a dying flame.

Beyond the wagon line, Til McLean faced the girl, so shaken by the thing that had happened to him that no words immediately came. The rising flames of the burning wagons laid a throbbing light on them and the explosions of tinder-dry wagon beds were like rifle shots striking close by. She looked up with desolation on her face and suddenly put her arms around him and clenched her fingers together as though never to let him go. Her body shuddered against him.

"I had to pay for it," he said. "Soon as the Indians hit, I knew that."

"You'll die. I won't ever see you again."

"No," he said, "I'll make out."

"It's so far," she said. "And if you get there, how will we ever meet?"

188

"At The Dalles," he said. "That's where the train reaches the river. I'll be there."

"Promise," she said.

"I swear it," he said. "I can do what's got to be done."

Then she let him go and he turned and walked toward the waiting horse within the circle. He climbed to the saddle and met Captain Whitney's glance.

"I wish you luck," said Captain Whitney.

McLean only nodded. His heels urged the horse across the circle and through the wagons, vanishing beyond the firelight. The crowd broke, men and women walking in dull silence toward their wagons and their beds.

Whitney joined Fitzpatrick. "Fitz," he said, "what chance has he got?"

"The odds are fifty-fifty he'll make the Snake without his hair lifted."

"What chance beyond the Snake?"

"If he makes the Snake alive, he'll be smart enough by then to go on through the rest of the way without any trouble."

"Let it be so," said Whitney and went on to the Halsey wagon.

His wife and daughter stood there, saying nothing. Both of them, he realized, hated him at the moment, and in such case there was nothing for him to say. He dropped to his blankets beneath the wagon. His wife would, in time, understand, but if Til McLean failed to reach Oregon his daughter would never forgive him, and that would be the final consequence of a young man's joke.

He pulled off his boots, drew the blanket over him. He had an hour's rest before daybreak, but found it difficult to sleep.

SECRET OF THE MALPAIS

BY RICHARD FERBER

The gold was his. All he had to do was go back and get it . . . back deep into the Apache country where gold fever ran high, turning White Man against Indian, White against White, brother against brother.

A DELL WESTERN   35c

LAST TRAIN TO BANNOCK

A NEW CLAYBURN WESTERN BY
AL CONROY

The trail from Parrish City to Bannock was the deadliest stretch in the West, plagued by man-hunting Apache raids, crippling blizzards, and gold-hungry white men hired to kill. Somewhere along this trail behind a mass of rocks, Clayburn crouched—waiting.

A Dell Book   *40c*

LUKE SHORT'S
BOLD RIDER

The story of a gunfighter named Poco who rode alone and lived by violence, so that others might live by the law

"If Poco was killed in Rincon, this town wouldn't stand a week. And all the land God ever made wouldn't be big enough for you to hide in if you killed him."

"I'm not asking you, Sheriff. I'm telling you. You'll get me Poco or spend the rest of your life on the dodge."

"It won't work, Mac. He'll get away because the jail hasn't been built yet that will hold him."

"Then kill him."

"How many guys have tried it—and where are they now?"

A DELL BOOK   **40c**

If you cannot obtain copies of this title at your local newsstand, just send the price (plus 10c per copy for handling and postage) to Dell Books, Box 2291, Grand Central Post Office, New York, N.Y. 10017. No postage or handling charge is required on any order of five or more books.